Wild Atlantic Anthology

Characters Along Ireland's Majestic Coast

Volume 1

Mary Heeran White

Published and Manufactured by Softwood Books

EU Responsible person: Maddy Glenn
Office 2, Wharfside House, Prentice Road, Stowmarket, Suffolk, IP14 1RD
www.softwoodbooks.com, hello@softwoodbooks.com

EU Rep:
Authorised Rep Compliance Ltd., Ground Floor, 71 Lower Baggot Street, Dublin, D02 P593, Ireland
www.arccompliance.com, info@arccompliance.com

A CIP catalogue record for this book is available from the British Library

ISBN: 978-1-3999-7414-1

This anthology transports readers through vivid tales, embracing the enthralling characters and landscapes along Ireland's wild coastline. Offering a captivating exploration of humanity's varied facets, showcasing the bond between people and their land, and the extraordinary tales that emerge when the two intersect. Each story embodies the untamed spirit of Ireland's coastline and its people.

Prepare to be enchanted by stories that resonate with you long after you've tuned the pages.

Dedicated to my parents Francie and Madge Heeran

Contents

Miracle of Baltimore

As the first rays of morning sun streamed through the farmhouse window, Jack Callaghan leaned forward to catch a glimpse of his cattle speckling the distant fields. The day had commenced under a blanket of rain, but a welcome break in the clouds ushered in a radiant brightness across the rugged hills and valleys that stood alongside the Atlantic. Spotting his neighbour, Finbar Murphy, assembling a hay rick, Jack's attention was drawn once more to Finbar's daughter, Lucy, diligently assisting her father in the meadow, just a stone's throw away.

Securing the scullery door and tucking the key beneath the geranium pot, Jack set forth along the road. His eyes lingered on Lucy, a young woman who had occupied his thoughts for an eternity. Through changing seasons and weather patterns, Jack's glimpses of Lucy had been sporadic. She worked diligently alongside her father on their meagre farm, nestled adjacent to Jack's more flourishing pastures on the outskirts of Baltimore.

As an only child whose parents had long passed, Jack had patiently awaited Lucy' evolution from child to woman, resolute in his desire to make her his wife. He had witnessed her gradual growth, her fiery red hair perpetually woven into twin French braids to her waist. It felt as though nature itself conspired to unite them—wafting scents of wildflowers entwined with the tang of the Atlantic, with fuchsia blossoms cascading around hedgerows.

Their furtive glances at each other resembled a game of catch with their eyes, bridging the physical expanse between them. Blessed with the stature of a footballer and the charisma of a silver-screen idol, Jack relished the jingle of coins in his pocket and the flourish of notes during his visits to the nearby towns of Skibbereen and Bantry. However, amidst numerous dalliances, his thoughts perpetually circled back to the girl next door.

Then, at last, Lucy turned nineteen, signalling the moment for Jack to openly court her. Yet, her father's consent came laced with a cautionary note. "Lucy has a fierce streak of independence," he warned. "She dreams of a future beyond the toil of her native West Cork. And she's a tad young for you, lad."

"I'm aware of the gap in years, Finbar, but I'd be both wise and foolish for her," replied Jack. "I'll court her right and take her places she's never seen, and she'll never want a day in her life. I'm a good catch with a decent farm and the means for a good life. Twenty years of a difference on a man's side is no harm once the bride has plenty of childbearing years."

"I won't argue with that. If that's what she wants that is."

"With any luck, we'll have enough children to bring some life into the place and help keep the school open in Baltimore for another while," said Jack.

"Now be warned, Lucy couldn't bake a cake to save her life," said Finbar. "But she's a good cook and handy at the mending and darning."

"Sure, not being able to bake a cake is an easy burden to bear for a man that never eats cake anyway," smiled Jack.

"Well, I'll leave it to you then," said Finbar, nodding his head in agreement. "She's down in the lower meadow."

Jumping to his feet, Jack was filled with a strength and conviction that he'd never felt before. Within seconds, the handsome devil with eyes black as charcoal and a mane of curled black hair bouncing off his tanned forehead was thundering through the sweet-smelling meadows towards the love of his life.

After a while, he found her, swinging her legs over the side of a riverbank at the bottom of the meadow, her youthful, angelic face bearing a small constellation of freckles. Having said so much with his eyes over the years, Jack found it hard to speak the words. After some idle chat about the weather and the haymaking, Jack took the plunge.

"So, Lucy, what would you say if I were to ask you to come to the Arcadia in town some night?" he asked.

"I don't know, rightly," she said.

"Sure, I could take you next Friday. Big Tom and the Mainliners are playing. It'll be a great night for your first time there."

Lucy glanced up at Jack, a glimmer of uncertainty in her eyes. "I'm not sure, Jack. I've never been to such a place before."

"Ah, it'll be grand! You'll have the time of your life," Jack assured her with an eager grin. "It's a dance hall, Lucy. People from all over gather there. Big Tom and the Mainliners play the best music in town. You'll love it, I swear."

She hesitated for a moment, fidgeting with a tuft of grass by the riverbank. "I don't know if it's right for me, Jack. My da thinks I should stay close to home."

"But you're your own person, Lucy," Jack said, leaning in closer. "It's about time you enjoyed yourself, experienced a bit of life outside these fields. I'll take care of you, I promise."

Lucy looked up at Jack, her eyes softening. "Alright, maybe I'll go with you. But just this once."

"Brilliant!" Jack exclaimed, his excitement evident. "I'll pick you up at seven on Friday. We'll have a great time, you'll see."

Lucy nodded with a shy smile before standing up, brushing hay off her skirt. "I should get back now. Da will be expecting me. Thank you, Jack."

As she started to walk away, Jack watched her go, his heart racing with anticipation. This was the start of something new, he was sure of it. With a grin plastered on his face, he made his way back home, already envisioning the evening ahead at the Arcadia with Lucy.

Friday evening couldn't come fast enough for Jack. Dressed in his most elegant tweed suit and white grandfather shirt, he drove his newly polished Mercedes to Lucy's door, careful to avoid the cocks and hens rushing round outside. He couldn't help but notice how rotten the thatch was on the roof, how it was patched with sheets of iron. Surely Lucy would want to cross the fields to his place? It was a palace by comparison.

Jack skilfully wove tales along the coastal journey, each bend revealing a breathtaking tapestry of lush hills and winding valleys. Along the rugged coastline, the Atlantic Ocean sprawled endlessly to their right, waves crashing against the cliffs with a rhythmic and eternal cadence, while Lucy remained quiet, taking in the sights.

He regaled her with local myths about the cliffs; stories whispered through generations about ancient giants frozen in time as stone sentinels overlooking the coast. Legends spoke of these giants shaping the shores with grand gestures, creating deep inlets and hidden coves for the games of Gods. Jack mentioned a nearby fairy fort, a ring of stones believed to serve as a portal to the Otherworld. Lucy chuckled at the notion but found herself captivated by the mythical tales. Jack watched with delight as her eyes sparkled, caught in the wonder where the lines between reality and fantasy blurred.

As they approached Baltimore, the charming village came into view, embraced by the quiet bay. Distant music from the Arcadia dance hall echoed through the air, their anticipation growing.

"They say the night's enchantment turns ordinary folk into extraordinary dancers," Jack said with a smile.

"I'm not much of a dancer," Lucy admitted.

"You'll be one before you know it," he assured her warmly.

Their evening at the dance hall was magical, and subsequent outings were equally delightful, each filled with precious moments. However, one day, Lucy spoke up about her aspirations.

"I've been thinking, Jack," she started. "I want to go to Dublin for a while. Get a job, make friends, and have some fun."

Lucy's unexpected decision to head to Dublin hurt Jack deeply, shattering his spirits. All those years of waiting for her to come of age, enduring longing glances exchanged over the barbed wire that separated their lands seemed to have held no value for her. Angry and bewildered, he sat upright.

"Why in God's name would someone like you want to traipse off to a big city like Dublin?" Jack blurted out, his words only fuelling Lucy's resolve.

"Well, there's a life outside these lands, Jack," she retorted, holding his gaze firmly. "I've read *The Country Girls*, and it's clear as day that Baba Brennan and Kate Brady had the time of their lives when they moved from the country to Dublin."

Lucy darted back across the fields, leaving Jack to grapple with her decision. He couldn't fathom why she'd choose the unknown of a big city over their potential union—a match that he deemed perfect with their combined assets of land, youth, and beauty. Feeling disillusioned, Jack pondered how wrong he had been about her intentions.

Baffled by her behaviour, Jack considered her actions. Would their marriage not be the perfect union, with a family to enjoy in the drearier years of ageing that would inevitably come? Him with his lush pastures and her with her youth and beauty. Dear God, to think she'd allowed him to bask all those years in a fool's paradise. And where did this leave his arrangement with Finbar? He could have sworn this was a done deal. How on earth had he got these notions so wrong?

The arrangement that he believed existed between their families now seemed a shattered dream.

Disillusioned, it became clear that him and Lucy were not of a similar mind; Jack never encountered Lucy again until her father's funeral two years later. Finbar's sudden death and all the sadness it brought to her and her mother left Jack thinking Lucy might be home to stay.

Later that day, however, it wasn't the sight of Finbar's corpse laid out in the parlour that took his breath away but rather the vision of Lucy, now in the prime of life, gracefully accepting his condolences with what he considered a renewed look of admiration in her eyes.

That night as the wails of caoiners echoed like banshees throughout the townland, Lucy sought comfort from Jack, burying her face in his strong, supportive shoulder. As she sobbed uncontrollably for her father, he laid his hand over hers, telling her not to worry, that he'd look after both her and her mother. Drawing a deep breath of contentment, Jack felt his marriage proposal could be renewed after the dust had settled.

As the months passed and Lucy no longer mentioned going back to Dublin, Jack's confidence grew. With renewed enthusiasm, he worked slavishly on the two farms, squaring off fields with pens and barbed wire fencing where cattle grazed contentedly.

One day, Jack finally gathered the courage to ask, "What kind of wedding would you like, Lucy?"

Her response, "With you," filled Jack's heart with joy.

Over time, he learned to appreciate the simplicity and steadfastness of Lucy's love, understanding that she had fallen for him after he'd pledged to take care of her and her mother at Finbar's funeral.

Their bond strengthened as they laboured together in the now flourishing fields. Yet, over the years without any children, Jack's concern grew, especially noticing Lucy's frequent visits to their local doctor and the hospital. Worry lines were etched on her once-beautiful face.

"It's nothing serious, don't fret," she'd reassure him after returning from what she referred to as her 'health checks' or 'women's matters'.

However, everything changed when Lucy casually mentioned that the hospital suggested he himself should go for tests. The realisation struck him suddenly, the weight of guilt settling heavily on his shoulders. The news shattered his spirit, eroding his passion faster than a fleeting mayfly. His inability to father a child deeply challenged his sense of manhood. Disheartened, their once-comfortable relationship began to chill, as if their mattress had turned to stone.

***

Jack pleaded with God, desperate for a child, but divine intervention seemed out of reach. The heavens remained silent, and the blessings of parenthood remained elusive.

He could almost envision the scoffs and mocking whispers at Jacob's Bar, the neighbours snickering as they pointed fingers at the man who once boasted of marrying a young bride and starting a large family.

The weight of shame became unbearable for Jack. After one too many drinks, he finally unleashed his pent-up guilt to local Sergeant John Donoghue. Donoghue possessed an uncanny ability to keep tabs on the happenings in West Cork, often preventing potential conflicts and crimes through his insightful tips.

As Jack revealed the nature of his situation, Donoghue proposed a solution that might offer respite from his agony.

"Have you heard of Seamus Feeney?" Donoghue inquired.

"I have, and none of it was good, as you well know," replied Jack.

"He's got a reputation for leaving women pregnant and disappearing when there's talk of the women putting on weight," Donoghue explained. "They call him 'hammer Feeney'."

"He's nothing but a scoundrel. His whole family is notorious for their reckless behaviour and carousing. Wasn't his father just the same? "Who'd want to associate with him?" Jack retorted.

"Well, it depends on what use you might have for him," Donoghue hinted cryptically.

Jack, perplexed by Donoghue's suggestion, questioned, "What use would that good-for-nothing layabout be to me, might I ask?"

"Well now, I'll leave you to figure that one out, Jack. With the reputation the man has, might he not be a solution to your problem?" With a slight smile, Donoghue bid Jack goodnight and departed.

Mulling over Donoghue's cryptic words, Jack lay awake in bed that night, only to jolt awake from slumber with a sudden realisation. The thought of Feeney being suggested as a solution, slipping into his bed, and impregnating his wife revolted him. It left him drenched in sweat, deeply offended at the idea, and viewing it as an insult to his virility. Determined to confront Donoghue, he likened the suggestion to nothing short of livestock insemination.

Despite his initial aversion, the idea lingered in Jack's mind, causing sleepless nights and ceaseless torment. However, proposing such an outlandish plan to his wife was inconceivable.

Jack distanced himself from Donoghue and his regular

visits to Jacob's Bar. However, fate led them to meet at a neighbour's burial in Bantry, where a conversation about Seamus Feeney took an unexpected turn.

"I heard Seamus Feeney hasn't long left in him," said Donoghue.

"Is that so?" replied Jack, perturbed by the conversation.

"Cancer. He won't see Easter," Donoghue revealed.

"That's an awful rumour," Jack retorted, still irritated by Donoghue's prior suggestion.

"Refusing treatment of any sort. He reckons he'd lose the Feeney magic if his fine head of black curls disappeared."

The next morning, Jack, during breakfast, cautiously broached the topic with Lucy about Seamus Feeney, attempting to hide his true feelings.

"Have you ever heard of Seamus Feeney?" he broached.

"I have indeed. Sure, there isn't a woman in the area who doesn't admire him," Lucy replied, unaware of the implications.

Feeling a surge of mixed emotions, Jack retorted, "You wouldn't mind a night with him then, I suppose?"

The shock on Lucy's face was immediate. Without a word, she stormed off, leaving Jack alone in the silent kitchen, a silence that persisted for weeks despite his attempts at conversation.

Filled with regret and frustration at his foolishness, Jack blamed himself for the rift in their marriage.

In the months that followed after the fallout of their conversation, Jack noticed a marked change in Lucy's appearance. Her once-pale complexion now glowed with a healthy radiance that brightened her face. Her skin, once dull and worn, appeared rejuvenated, now boasting a fresh vitality that hadn't been there before. He couldn't help but notice how her cheeks gained a colour and her eyes, once tired, now sparkled with a newfound liveliness. She seemed to bloom with an inner contentment.

Lucy put on a bit of weight, but it was not the weight of sadness or distress. It was a healthy and comforting increase, one that added softness to her features. Her figure, while fuller, appeared to give her confidence that Jack hadn't seen in her for quite some time. She had an air of contentment about her that pleased him.

As Jack observed these changes, he couldn't help

but notice the renewed energy in Lucy's step, the contagious smile that adorned her face. She seemed at peace, content in a way that she hadn't been in a while. However, despite these striking transformations, Jack couldn't fathom the reason behind Lucy's newfound happiness.

One morning, as they sat across from each other at the kitchen table, Lucy, her eyes gleaming with happiness, looked at Jack with a serene expression. There was a moment of silence, a palpable tension lingering between them before Lucy took a deep breath.

"Jack," she started, her voice carrying a mix of nervousness and excitement. "I have something to tell you." Her hand gently rested on her abdomen, an unconscious gesture that revealed her secret before the words escaped her lips.

A flicker of realisation crossed Jack's face, his eyes widening in disbelief as he connected the dots. His gaze shifted to Lucy's glowing face and then to her abdomen, where her hand had instinctively moved.

Before Lucy could utter another word, Jack sat there, struck by a sudden realisation. The transformation he had noticed in her appearance, the glow in her eyes, and the gentle weight gain — it all made sense now.

A mixture of emotions flooded Jack — surprise, disbelief, and an overwhelming sense of joy. As the truth sank in, a warm smile spread across his face, mirroring Lucy's, and he reached out to hold her hand. In that moment, no words were needed. They shared a silent understanding, an unspoken confirmation of the new life that was on the way — a life that would forever change their world.

***

As Easter arrived, fulfilling John Donoghue's prediction, a hearse solemnly made its way down Roscarbery Road, carrying Seamus Feeney to his final resting place in the local cemetery. Among the crowd paying their respects were Jack and Lucy, cradling their baby boy in their arms.

As Feeney's coffin was gently lowered into the ground, a sense of closure washed over Jack. Any lingering resentment he harboured towards the man dissipated. With his gaze fixed on his son, a tiny bundle with bright green eyes and a hint of red in his hair, Jack's heart swelled with love, a tear of sheer joy glistening in his eye.

Captivated by the innocence mirrored in his son's expression, reminiscent of the spark in Lucy's eyes when they first locked gazes across their adjoining fields, Jack felt an overwhelming rush of emotions. Suddenly, the sacrifices Lucy had made to bring happiness to their lives became clear to him.

Reaching out, Jack gently squeezed Lucy's hand, his touch conveying a flood of unspoken gratitude and affection. In response, Lucy squeezed his hand back, a tender gesture laden with a world of understanding and shared emotion.

As they prepared to leave, Sergeant Donoghue eyed them with a hint of playful knowing. With a twinkle in his eye, he watched as they walked away, knowing they had found solace in enduring traditions and whimsical local rituals.

Donegal Twins

Waking up in an unfamiliar setting, Danny McDaid blinked away the haze clouding his vision. The narrow bed he lay on felt confining, its stiff, striped sheets embracing him like a captive. A faded blue eiderdown lay tightly tucked around him, adding to his sense of restraint. His head throbbed dully, and a weight anchored his left leg. A dryness gripped his mouth, leaving him yearning for a drink.

Uncertain of how much time had passed, he lay there, immobilised, grappling with mounting apprehension. Eventually, the muffled sounds of heavy breathing nearby broke the shallow doze he'd drifted into. Suddenly, a hand yanked aside the smoky curtain veiling his bed.

"How are you feeling today, Mister McDaid?" chirped a burly nurse, her presence an unexpected intrusion. Danny, bewildered by her identity, couldn't fathom how she knew him at all.

"They've done a great job on you over the past days, getting you all cleaned up," she continued. "You were in an awful state. Bad bout of pneumonia. You've slept well since you've been here."

Grabbing a chart that hung at the end of his bed,

the nurse scribbled something on it.

"All being well, the doctor'll probably discharge you tomorrow," she added, replacing the chart, and turning to face him. "You're a lucky man, you know. Your brother found you unconscious in a remote field somewhere and brought you here. You must have been there an exceptionally long time; you were near death's door."

Utterly confused, and despite his weakened state, Danny asked for his clothes, feeling the urgent need to take control of the situation. But the nurse was having none of it.

Raising her hand with the authority of a Sergeant Major, she announced sharply, "You're in the workhouse, and you're going nowhere until I say so. You'll get your clothes as soon as the doctor gives you the all-clear. Don't worry; if tests show you haven't got TB, you won't be kept here much longer."

Frightened by the unknown and the suffocating smell of Jays Fluid, Danny struggled to get out of bed, but his body felt like lead. Pulling himself up with earnest effort, he tried to grab hold of the nurse, but she stepped back, evading him easily. Frustrated, he swiped at thin air violently, shouting, "Get my fucking clothes and stop lying to me! My brother didn't bring me here."

"You're disoriented, Mister McDaid. Understandably so. But please, sit back and relax. If you try to grab me again like that, you won't need discharge papers. I'll kick you out of here myself."

Realising he hadn't the strength to protest, he slumped back onto the hard pillow and closed his eyes in resignation. Within seconds, his mind drifted back in time as he tried to piece together the events that had brought him here.

He recalled the postman dropping off a letter from the local solicitor requesting that he and his brother, Paddy, attend his office for the reading of their parents' will. Aware of the formality of the occasion, he'd worn his best suit. Danny recalled going with confidence of the outcome, his father having already promised him the rich uplands into which he'd poured endless months of hard labour, cutting, cultivating, and draining. His brother Paddy had long since abandoned the home farm, instead deciding on studying at university, finding a teaching post afterwards, an achievement his parents were enormously proud of.

Arriving at Doherty's Solicitors in Carndonagh on a dreary November morning, Danny was taken aback to find his brother already there, wearing an unsettling expression. The elderly solicitor perched his glasses at the bridge of his nose, carefully unfurled documents, and proceeded to read the will out loud. As the words echoed in the room, Danny's shock turned to anger.

"Paddy shall inherit the uplands (Folio 9763) and Danny the rocky area (Folio 4836). Any remaining savings shall be distributed equally between Danny and Paddy after payment for the erection of a family headstone," the solicitor announced.

Stunned, Danny sat frozen, his mind racing. The eighty-acre upland farm he'd toiled on for years was supposed to be his. His father had promised it to him, acknowledging Danny's early departure from school to help work the land. What had prompted this sudden change? And Paddy, already employed with a steady income at the local school, was to inherit the less fertile land. It made no sense.

Beside his brother, Danny's heart sank as the solicitor finished the reading. Outraged, unable to contain his frustration, he shouted, "This is wrong! The uplands were promised to me!"

Silence gripped the office. Paddy, eager to finalise the matter, expressed gratitude to Mr. Doherty. Danny, growing more exasperated, spoke up. "When was this change made?"

Nervously shuffling through papers, the solicitor

hesitated before replying, "October 1967."

The date triggered suspicion. Danny vividly remembered his father's will from 1965. He recalled his father's words: "Paddy is well settled now. You need the uplands to survive." The sudden change in the will fuelled Danny's anger.

Paddy attempted to placate Danny, saying, "You've got the bigger piece of the farm anyway."

"That's utter nonsense, and you know it!" Danny snapped before his rage exploded. Without warning, he lashed out, landing a forceful blow on Paddy, sending him crashing to the floor.

In the chaos that followed, the solicitor called for the authorities, and Danny, consumed with horror at what he'd done, fled the scene. Racing through Carndonagh's streets, fear gripped him. Fleeing the scene on foot, he eventually approached Trawbreaga Bay. Relieved he wasn't being followed, he cut across the fields, haunted by the possibility of having committed an unfathomable act against his own brother.

**

Weeks later, awaiting discharge from the workhouse, Danny still struggled to comprehend his brother's actions. Paddy seemed to him privileged in every way, yet he had deprived him of his rightful inheritance, a betrayal Danny found incomprehensible from someone that shared the same blood. The hurt lingered, for it wasn't just about the land; it was about the principles of fairness and brotherly love instilled by their parents.

His time in the workhouse provided solitude for reflection. Danny delved deep into the past, trying to unearth when Paddy's disdain for him had taken root. The memory of his first day at school pierced through. Eager for some comfort in an unfamiliar environment, Danny had hoped Paddy's presence might offer solace. Instead, he overheard his brother disdaining him, branding him as 'the one with the hare lip'. The mockery from Paddy and his friends relentlessly tormented him throughout his school years, leaving him with a lasting lack of confidence.

Paddy had a nasty cohort of friends who enjoyed nothing more than mocking him, goading him at every opportunity, knowing his embarrassment would result in his freckled face growing the same colour as his flame-red hair. Too ashamed to retaliate, the torment continued throughout national school until Paddy left for the nearby vocational one.

Danny's resulting lack of confidence left him too

nervous to leave his local surroundings in fear of finding himself in another place where he might be unable to find a job or make friends. He remained in lonely desolation, hard work on the farm being his only satisfaction. Trapped in the same sorry existence for the past thirty-two years, after giving up school to work the land, he realised he had nothing to show for his sad existence. Worst of all, he was painfully aware that in this remote corner of Ireland, where the land meets the sea in a ceaseless battle, his life, his love, and his despair could vanish without a trace. The landscape that had helped shape him could just as easily swallow him. This stark realisation heightened the depths of his despair as he lay brooding in the workhouse awaiting discharge.

Yet he longed to return home to the ever-changing weather, from calm and clear to wild and stormy. For some unknown reason, he missed the familiar untamed world of rugged cliffs, relentless winds, and the sweeping vistas of the sea. It was where his heart longed to be.

Long hours of solitude brought on a sudden rush of memories flooding back, piercing through the fog of his mind. Finally, he vividly recalled the unexpected encounter with his horse — Daisy. His desperation to regain strength matched the intensifying self-loathing that surged within him. The memories resurfaced from the fateful morning when Daisy vanished, casting a shadow upon his thoughts and deepening his disdain, particularly toward his brother.

He recalled the scene clearly from that fateful morning. Having rattled the latch of the wrought-iron gate leading to the haggard before grabbing a ripened apple from a nearby tree to entice her to him, listening to the call of the corncrake echoing across the rugged fields of Inishowen, he waited for his horse to amble towards him for his reward. Concerned at not seeing Daisy or hearing the familiar sound of her neighing, he called out her name more loudly, then began a search. Some hours later, barely pausing for breath, he'd scoured all the surrounding fields, promising apples and bags of hay should she return. But there was only silence around Trawbreaga Bay, leaving Danny with an overwhelming feeling of discomfort. Familiar November clouds gathered, and winter's early darkness had begun to settle as winds over the Atlantic howled furiously.

Struggling against the unyielding forces of nature, he staggered through the harsh landscape to find her, the biting winds and the unrelenting downpour amplified his growing dread. Amid the enveloping darkness, a startling dart to his body disrupted the thunderous crash of the Atlantic waves against the shore.

His chest tightened, suffocating him, and he crumbled onto the pale sands, gasping for breath, the taste of salt and grit filling his mouth.

Underneath his trembling fingers, he sensed something that ignited a primal fear within him. The object was soft, with a peculiar texture, unlike anything he had felt before. As he looked down, his fingertips met an ear — a familiar one. It was Daisy's ear, his beloved companion he had cared for with unwavering devotion.

Shaken with dread, he extended his hand further, brushing against the hand-crafted halter. The realisation struck him hard. This was Daisy, her head and neck emerging from the salt marshes. Once adorned with a flowing mane, now reduced to a faint wisp on her skeletal frame.

"Daisy ... My dear Daisy, no, ah no!" he choked out, his voice trembling with sorrow.

Overwhelmed by grief, Danny wept uncontrollably. With a heavy heart, he collapsed, pressing his face against his beloved horse's head, the unforgiving landscape silently witnessing the heart-wrenching tragedy unfold before it.

***

After his discharge from the workhouse Danny emerged with newfound strength, physically and mentally prepared to return home. However, his homecoming was marked by a stark transformation in his perspective. The once-charming, thatched cottage, which had held his heart, now seemed to enclose him within a stifling solitude. Its whitewashed walls, once comforting, now appeared bare and imprisoning. In a matter of mere weeks, the modest comforts he'd once cherished meant little to him.

Unable to settle, an unrelenting desire for retribution consumed him. The loneliness without his beloved Daisy became unbearable. He became fixated on ending the ceaseless torment that his brother had inflicted upon him throughout the years. Driven by this obsession, he embarked toward the barn, clutching the very gun he'd once used for mink hunting. Two bullets, hidden within the pockets of his worn hunting jacket, signalled his unwavering determination.

His path led him across the fields to Paddy's house, where anger, frustration, and years of pent-up resentment boiled within him. As he reached the doorstep, his emotions simmering, he found the house empty. Without hesitation, he sought refuge in the barn, knowing Paddy's predictable nature would lead him to park his car beside the creaking door.

Moments later, the distant hum of an approaching engine triggered Danny's resolve. As the car lurched to a halt, just as he had foreseen, Danny initiated his plan. He rattled empty milk buckets, creating a ruckus designed to lure his brother into the barn.

Paddy, responding to the noise, dashed into the barn with anticipation of a stray dog or a marauding mink. However, he came to an abrupt halt, shocked by the sight of a gun levelled directly at him. Caught off-guard, he stumbled backward, the colour draining from his face.

"What ... what in the world are you doing? You should be at the workhouse recovering from pneumonia. How on earth did they let you out?" Paddy stammered, clearly unnerved.

"Your concern is touching," Danny retorted bitterly.

"Please, put that gun away, Danny. You've scared me half to death. Come inside and I'll pour you a whiskey."

"A whiskey? When have you ever invited me into your house, let alone offered me a whiskey?" Danny's grip on the gun tightened, watching Paddy cautiously as he tried to edge away from the line of fire.

Paddy's tone took on a conciliatory note. "Danny, let's end this petty rivalry, shall we? We should have stopped before it escalated to this point, even before you struck me in the solicitor's office. I could've pressed charges, but I didn't."

Your mercy is truly overwhelming," Danny sneered.

"No, I mean it," Paddy pleaded.

"You made my father change his will. You were always a greedy bastard. But why, why did you have to destroy my Daisy?"

"Ah, Daisy ... You think I had something to do with her?" Paddy's voice wavered as he attempted to explain.

Danny's voice grew colder. "Yes, I found her. You believed I never would, didn't you? You thought you could hide her forever."

"Her wandering into my fields ... I couldn't take it anymore. She acted like she owned the place. Trampling my entire vegetable plot. She turned my patch into a bloody battlefield! I've spent weeks planting and trimming, and now it looks like a scene out of a war film."

Danny halted his accusations, tears streaming down his face. "She deserved better. You took her from me in the cruellest way possible just to hurt me."

Paddy, sensing Danny's growing fury, began to plead desperately, bowing his head and begging for mercy. But it was far too late for reconciliation. Danny pulled the trigger, and a deafening blast reverberated throughout the barn. Minutes later, another gunshot followed.

Time itself suspended in that haunting moment.

The barn door remained bolted shut. The old, rusted gate, once a portal for Daisy's lively trot towards her adoring owner, stood frozen in time, its hinges corroded by neglect. It was a silent monument to bygone days, a poignant symbol of the family's fading legacy in the heart of Inishowen.

Earthy Adoration

Awakening from a fitful slumber, Caitlyn Hogan emerged from beneath the sheets and pulled back the curtains in her dimly lit room. The solitude of her cottage nestled in the foothills of Mullaghmore was tinged with an unsettling sense of disquiet. Peering through the window, the night appeared undisturbed, yet an eerie sensation lingered. Draping a shawl around her shoulders to ward off the autumn chill, she sensed the unnerving stillness that enveloped her home. Only the haunting melody of a distant curlew pierced the silence, echoing across the vast limestone expanse of the Burren.

Six solemn chimes from the grandfather clock in the hallway marked the beginning of her daily ritual, a routine marred by growing concern for her husband, Tony. Throughout their forty-year marriage, Tony had seldom been ill except for occasional severe indigestion, which typically confined him to bed. However, his slow recovery this time weighed heavily on her mind.

Venturing through the yard to gather turf, she moved among the dandelions and clover, the distant sound of waves crashing against the shore serving as a backdrop to her thoughts. Filling her basket in the barn, she shivered in the cold, the dawn fog hanging like a damp veil over the nearby turloughs, blanketing the landscape under the moonlight. She grew annoyed by thoughts of her nosy neighbour, Nellie, knowing she peered through her nearby window at every move she made. Nellie's curiosity had spiked since Tony's abrupt halt in his daily routine two days previously. Yet, Caitlyn remained resolute in maintaining distance, determined to provide a tranquil haven for her husband's recovery.

In the distance, the imposing Cliffs of Moher emerged, extending into the sea. Through the mist, the formless shape of the O'Brien Tower was barely visible, as Caitlyn silently willed for Tony's resurgence from his slumber, hoping against hope for his recovery. She beseeched the mythical figures woven into the ancient legends of the Burren to intervene and save him.

Caitlyn and Tony had been childhood sweethearts since their days at Ballinalackin National School. Their future as spouses had been evident to everyone, given their adjacent family farms. In the summer of 1956, Caitlyn's mother passed away, and it was then they decided to marry. On Tony's twenty-first birthday, he presented his mother's wedding ring, slipping it onto Caitlyn's finger with quiet determination. Their union was cemented without grand proclamations of love. An unbreakable bond had already taken root between them.

In the early years of their marriage, Caitlyn grappled with an overwhelming fear of intimacy. Unsure how to shed her shyness and unease regarding physical affection she dreaded the potential discomfort or pain that might accompany her efforts to satisfy Tony's desires. Her apprehension made the thought of having children repugnant, causing her to shun Tony's advances entirely. The ensuing lack of intimacy between them bred frustration, eventually leading to a distance that transformed their relationship, leaving them estranged in that aspect. Affection waned, reducing even comforting embraces or tender kisses to memories.

However, beyond their strained intimacy, their life together was content. Their marriage vows stood firm, binding them to care for each other through thick and thin. They engaged in inconsequential conversations about neighbours' passing, brief discussions about stolen cattle or missing sheep, and infrequent outings to the horse fair in Spancil Hill, together with weekly shopping trips forming the mundane fabric of their daily existence.

Grabbing hold of her prayer book, she called on the

Sacred Heart, Saint Anthony, Saint Brigid, and all the saints to rid Tony of his indigestion. "Rest now," she murmured over him. "It'll blow over, Tony."

She tried to feel his pulse but didn't know what a normal pulse felt like. But his was slow as a hearse. Frightened, she wondered whether she should call a doctor or a priest when she thought she heard Tony breathing, or at least letting out a sigh.

Deep in contemplation, Caitlyn was taken aback by the sound of a car driving up to the cottage. Setting aside her attempt to prop up the pillows around Tony, who lay motionless in bed, she hurried downstairs to greet the unexpected visitor.

"Good day, Mrs. Hogan," greeted the local Garda Sergeant cheerfully as she opened the door.

"I'm Sergeant Foley."

"I know who you are."

"Can I come in for a minute?"

Guiding him to the dimly lit parlour, unused since her mother's wake, Caitlyn's discomfort grew as the cold air hit her upon opening the door.

"What brings you here?" she inquired after they settled.

"Your neighbour reported your husband's absence, and I wanted to make sure everything was alright," he said, smiling.

"He's not absent," Caitlyn retorted, feeling indignant. "It's a pity the neighbour didn't learn to mind her own business. She's causing trouble where there is none.

"So, is he here now?"

"He might be."

"May I talk to him?"

As the sergeant took out his notebook, Caitlyn felt anger simmer at her neighbour's intrusion into her privacy.

"As you know, farmers don't lounge around the house. Tony's always occupied on the land."

"Understood." The sergeant jotted down notes. "Has he ever stayed away for more than twenty-four hours before?"

"He might have over the years. I can't recall that far back."

"Where do you think he might have gone?"

"To the fields. Wherever he roams, he always returns."

"Mrs. Hogan, do excuse me, but are you and your husband getting along? Any major disagreements lately that could have led him to leave?"

Shocked by such probing questions about her private life, Caitlyn reacted impulsively. Jumping to her feet, she grabbed a walking stick, raising it in fury. Sergeant Foley, taken aback by her sudden action, moved swiftly to protect himself.

"Get out of this house," Caitlyn shouted. "Who are you to question me based on a neighbour's gossip? Get out this instant!"

Peering through the porch window to be certain Foley had gone, she trembled with fear and tension. Suddenly she felt dizzy. Collapsing to the floor, she released a torrent of pent-up tears. The sergeant's visit instigated a dreadful thought in her mind — the possibility of Tony's demise.

***

Thankful that he was nearing his parked car, Foley reflected on how he despised the system that had brought him to investigate Tony Hogan's disappearance following a neighbour's report. Vowing never to arrive in the same situation again, of having to question a weakened old lady in such a suspicious manner, he couldn't overlook the terror in Mrs Hogan's eyes when she'd understood his line of questioning.

Sheltered in his car, Foley carefully navigated the twisting boreen, coming to a gradual halt as the piercing wails emanated from Hogan's house. Worried that he had caused Mrs Hogan such grief, he drove to the neighbouring house who had reported Tony's disappearance.

"Strange pair, the two of them," Nellie O'Neill muttered, casting a wary glance toward the Hogans' house. "Caitlyn never cared much for visitors. She'd rather be left alone. Always been like that. Not much conversation between them, yet they're as tight as can be. Oddballs, really! Mind you, Sergeant, if you were in a spot of bother and needed Tony's help, he'd be there in a heartbeat. And poor Caitlyn, loyal to him like an old hound, but a peculiar one at that."

Sergeant Foley listened attentively.

"She told us that if there's smoke coming out of her chimney, she's obviously alive and not to bother her. She makes sure that the fire is alight at an unearthly hour of the morning before any of us are up. That'll tell you, Sergeant."

"To each his own, Nellie. We all have our peculiarities. So why do you think he's disappeared then?"

"Tony Hogan leaves the house and heads for the fields at 6.30 am every day, rain or shine, for as long as I've moved into the area. You could set your clock by his timing. He hasn't done it over the past days so there's something wrong for sure. No one has seen him in the fields either."

"He could be sick or even have a dose of flu," replied Foley, reaching for his notebook again, more hopeful this time.

"There's no sighting of him, I tell you, Sergeant. It's as if he disappeared into thin air."

"It's nothing more than a hunch, Nellie?"

"It's more than that, Sergeant. It's not right. I can sense there's something wrong."

"It's not enough for me, I'm afraid. For the moment, anyway, Mrs O'Neill."

"I've had my suspicions before, Sergeant, and I've usually been right."

In the past, Nellie's ability to provide the local station with well-informed local surveillance of warring neighbours and cattle theft in the locality had proved useful to them.

"So, you'll keep an eye on the property and let me know if you see anything unusual going on."

"I will indeed, Sergeant. I'm always glad to help the guards with anything."

***

Meanwhile, Caitlyn, wiping away tears, contemplated her next steps. Recollecting the morning she'd last prepared Tony's breakfast, she shuddered, suddenly gripped by fear. The unease grew as she realised the untouched tea and the buttered slice of brown bread remained on his bedside locker. Climbing upstairs, she approached Tony's bed side again. She found him lying still, his face gaunt and distant, staring at the ceiling. Feeling a chill, she shook him, yet there was no response.

Panicked, she debated whether to call a doctor or priest, unsure of Tony's condition. Rushing to the parochial house, Caitlyn hoped Father O'Brien could offer guidance.

Seated across from the local priest, she poured out her heart, confiding to the priest about Tony's prolonged slumber of two days, her initial assumption of indigestion tragically mistaken, now fearing that he had passed away quietly in his sleep.

"Tony's always been there for me," she confided,

fighting back tears. "But when he stayed in bed, I tried to connect, to show him I was there. I cried, Father. I never cry. And today, I said something I should have said long ago. Something I'll regret not saying."

"And what is that, Caitlyn?" asked the priest gently.

"That I love him," she whispered. "I never said it. I should have, but it was hard. He couldn't either. Those words weren't in his vocabulary. But I knew. He loved me and the land. And I loved him. He lived for us both. I should have told him."

"Don't dwell on regrets, Caitlyn," consoled Father O'Brien. "Love was in your actions, and that's what matters."

Standing up, he added, "We should go back to the house now, Caitlyn. I've a few things to collect here at the Sacristy. I'll meet you there in a few minutes."

On her return, Caitlyn, wearied with worry, climbed into bed beside Tony. Holding her rosary beads, she nestled closer to him than ever, feeling an inexplicable light wash over her as she closed her eyes. In that moment, she imagined hearing Tony calling her name. "Caitlyn ... I'm home."

***

Arriving later, the priest quietly entered the bedroom

and called out to Caitlyn but received no response. Alarmed, he hurried to the bed. Both Tony and Caitlyn lay motionless.

Just then, a light seemed to drift through the window as if a switch had been turned on deep in the heart of the hills outside. It was the most spectacular light the priest had ever seen, creating a peculiar kind of harmony in the room.

Caitlyn, with an expression of serene peace, seemed to gaze beyond, as a faint light cast a gentle blue glow into the room.

Father O'Brien performed the last rites, sensing a profound connection between their spirits and the natural world around them, reaffirming his belief that those who are intertwined with nature have boundless ties in the spiritual realm.

Last Chance Saloon

Padraig Moriarity grappled with his rebellious beard, wielding the razor against the unruly tufts that adorned his face. The result wasn't a precise shave but a painful gash on his chin, a vivid mark that told the tale of a morning ritual gone awry.

In a quest for something to stop the bleeding, he turned away from the unforgiving mirror. The disarray that met his eyes mirrored not only the crumbling bungalow snug in the heart of the Kerry countryside but also the state of his own life. The hollow rooms echoed with emptiness, the walls murmured stories of decay, all of it a poignant reflection of a life that had splintered and crumbled since the departure of his parents.

Minutes later, a hastily applied strip of newspaper attempting to stifle the bleeding, his bleary eyes stared through the fly-spattered windscreen as his worn-out Morris Minor rattled down the narrow path leading to Meadow Court Nursing Home.

With scant change in his pocket, his savings exhausted on fuel, he embarked on an unwanted journey—to visit his uncle Jimmy and reclaim an inheritance that was rightfully his.

Driving through the mist-shrouded Ring of Kerry, Padraig was plagued by guilt for his long neglect of Uncle Jimmy, who'd been a haven of kindness throughout his youth. Memories flooded in of birthdays and sacraments, with Uncle Jimmy always there, handing over a shiny coin. Was his negligence the cause of Jimmy altering his will? Deep down, Padraig knew the fault lay with him. And now, he faced the daunting task of righting his wrongdoings.

A sheen of sweat formed on his forehead, not from physical exertion but from the fear of rejection by an ailing uncle who might not even recognise him after years of absence. As he approached his destination, an impulse to turn back tugged at him, but his dire financial straits kept him moving forward. Recapturing his uncle's affection and the substantial inheritance could ignite family discord, even a feud, but Padraig saw no alternative. He was desperate. His finances had become an incessant leak, haemorrhaging like a burst pen since the original will, with tales of his drinking and squandering reaching Uncle Jimmy's ears. Padraig was annoyed that his sister, Sheila, after poisoning Jimmy's mind with stories of his wastefulness, ultimately became the sole beneficiary of his will. To make matters worse, she was married to Sergeant Donnie Walsh, a man with an eagle eye, seemingly waiting for any misstep Padraig might take.

When his electricity was cut off, Padraig paid no heed; he could stumble to his bedroom in the dark. When the roof leaked, he placed a bucket beneath. As his land sale money vanished, he borrowed from neighbours, who eventually shunned him. But the ultimate blow came when the shopkeeper and local publican refused him credit.

As his car rattled like a machine gun, trailing blue smoke, Padraig understood the weight of his mission: to convince his uncle of his worthiness to reinstate his inheritance and to surpass the matron guarding the nursing home. Rumours had circulated about her isolation tactics, manipulating residents out of their assets with her guided stroke of a pen.

Catching his bloodshot eyes in the rearview mirror, Padraig's anxiety soared. Years of daily spirits and pints had aged him prematurely, leaving a ruddy, dishevelled countenance. Hopefully, his ninety-year-old uncle wouldn't recognise the haggard state he was in.

An hour later, facing the nursing home's entrance, Padraig longed for a gulp of poitín to steady his nerves. Glancing apprehensively over his shoulder, he fumbled in the inside pocket of his tattered coat, retrieving a small bottle for a bracing gulp of the potent liquid. Then, with a trembling finger, he reached to ring the bell.

The door swung open with alarming speed, jolting Padraig backward. A robust woman stood before him, her gaze sharp and unwavering. "I'm the matron here. What do you want?" she demanded, her tone curt.

Her scrutinising eyes bore into Padraig, assessing his dishevelled appearance—the unkempt grey hair, the crumpled overcoat, the piece of newspaper stuck to his chin, his rosacea nose brighter than a ripened strawberry. The matron's disdain was palpable, and Padraig's attempt at composure seemed futile.

"Good day, Mam," he managed, attempting to maintain calm. "I've come to visit my uncle, Jimmy Moriarity."

The matron's gaze intensified. "Jimmy Moriarity? And who might you be? You've not graced this door since he arrived."

Struggling to assert himself, Padraig forged on. "I'm his nephew. It's been a while, but I want to make amends. He was always my favourite uncle. I've been remiss in not visiting."

"Jimmy won't be receiving visitors," she snapped. "Our policy requires prior notice and consent. Good day."

As the door began to close, Padraig halted it with his foot. "Please, can you inform him I'm here? I'm unwell and wish to pay what might be my final visit."

The words slipped out before he could reconsider. The matron remained unimpressed, eyeing him critically, her chin quivering slightly as she leaned closer as if to smell his breath. Unexpectedly, she turned and strode down the dimly lit corridor, leaving the door ajar. Hesitantly, he followed her gaze, observing her muttering something about "parasites" and sucking the remains of relatives' fortunes.

Padraig felt the weight of her disdain and suspected her intentions to thwart his plans if the rumours about her greed held any truth.

Stepping inside, he noticed unopened letters on the frayed doormat and a faint aroma of stale food clinging to the worn velvet curtains that veiled the windows. The noon Angelus bells rang, startling him. It wasn't fear that made him shiver but the cold and hunger gnawing at him relentlessly. Nausea threatened to overwhelm him, but a creaking door pulled his focus, and the matron appeared, gesturing for him to follow.

"Ah, relatives emerge as swift as snakes," she muttered to herself, her tone tinged with cynicism, leading Padraig forward.

The sting of the matron's words lingered in Padraig's mind, but he pressed on with a resolve born of necessity. He had to pursue his mission, despite the woman's provocations. Following her lead, he moved down the corridor until they reached a row of beds occupied by elderly men, their forms fragile and hauntingly familiar.

Among them lay a figure that bore a striking resemblance to Uncle Jimmy, albeit much frailer than Padraig remembered. As their eyes locked, emotions flooded Padraig's heart, bringing forth a wave of guilt that rendered him speechless. His uncle, now alert, peered at him with a glint of recognition amidst the fog of his aged mind.

Without wasting a moment, Padraig pulled a stool closer and seated himself by the bed. "I'm delighted to see you, Uncle Jimmy," he said, his voice tinged with both relief and desperation.

His uncle remained silent, gazing at him as if he didn't really know who he was.

Sensing the matron could return at any moment to thwart his efforts, Padraig knew he needed to prize him away from her clutches and rebuild the rapport he'd once enjoyed with the man before him. "Uncle Jimmy, I'm Padraig, your nephew. Will you come for a drive with me? Sure, it would do you a power of good to get out of this Godforsaken place for a while."

Uncle Jimmy's response was tentative, his focus wavering. "I won't budge without my meal. It's almost teatime, and I can't miss it, or I'll only get dried crackers for the rest of the day."

"I can return later," Padraig proposed.

"Agreed. We can go and see how your place is looking," Uncle Jimmy replied, his eyes reflecting a distant yet cautious trust.

Padraig's heart swelled with a mixture of relief and apprehension, taken aback by the fact that his uncle expressed such a keen interest in viewing his lands. As Padraig hurriedly left the nursing home, eager to plan before returning for his uncle, the absence of cattle or land to showcase troubled him.

Taking another slug of poitín to strengthen his resolve, Padraig arrived back an hour later and helped his feeble uncle into his clapped-out Morris Minor. He had a plan in his head. Instead of bringing him to his run-down farm in Cappamore, he'd decided to take him to a neighbouring farm stretching from Ahane in East Kerry to Dromdoory in the west, the best in the locality, with lush fields, a fine herd of grazing cattle, and new fencing and drainage. Then he'd convince him it was his. Padraig was sure his uncle would be mightily impressed by a sight matched only by the glorious twin-pinnacle crag of Selig Michael in the background.

Arriving at the neighbouring farm, Padraig presented the sweeping fields and robust livestock to his uncle, painting a compelling picture of his own triumphs. He narrated stories of toil and dedication, attributing the farm's prosperity to his supposed efforts. The glorious local surroundings added an air of authenticity to his tale, concealing the grim reality of his own dilapidated homestead.

As Padraig guided Uncle Jimmy around the farm, his explanations flowed with confidence, and his uncle listened attentively. Driving past the picturesque landscape, Padraig gloated over the property, orchestrating a tale of fabricated ownership as if weaving a spell.

Yet, as they travelled, Padraig felt the weight of his deception heavy on his shoulders. He was leading his uncle down a fabricated path, indulging in an elaborate fiction. Guilt crept in momentarily but seeing the glint of admiration in his uncle's eyes, Padraig swallowed hard, convincing himself that this was the only way to have his uncle change his will back to his name.

However, Padraig's confidence in his deception masked the tumultuous storm brewing within Uncle Jimmy's mind. The facade of the neighbouring farm's grandeur had been an elaborate mirage, and Jimmy, though weakened by age, was not deceived by Padraig's scheme.

Returning to the nursing home later, Padraig was elated, convinced he had successfully secured Uncle Jimmy's approval. The silence was an affirmation, confirming his belief that his uncle now saw him as a deserving heir to his legacy. Or so he believed.

The peacefulness of the nursing home ward was interrupted by the sound of a frail cough. Uncle Jimmy, seated on his bed, gazed out of the window, his expression a mixture of contemplation and resignation. Padraig, who stood nearby, anxiously waited for a word of approval, a sign that his deceit had been successful.

With a sudden clarity, Jimmy turned to Padraig, his voice feeble but filled with resolve. "Padraig, I appreciate the effort, I truly do. But no matter how convincing your tale, I can discern between fact and fiction. The farm you showed me isn't yours."

Padraig's heart sank. He tried to interject, to salvage his plan, but Jimmy raised his hand, silencing him. "I have neither the time nor the patience for more lies, lad. It saddens me to see the path you've chosen. I wish things were different, but I cannot change the reality of the situation."

Tears welled up in Padraig's eyes. He felt exposed, vulnerable, and deeply regretful. His attempts to deceive his uncle had only further deepened the divide between them.

Uncle Jimmy continued, his voice soft yet firm. "You've become entangled in a web of desperation, Padraig. Your choices have led you down a troubled path. The inheritance wasn't a promise but an opportunity to help you find your way. But you have to have honesty and integrity."

Padraig's shoulders sagged under the weight of his uncle's words. He had hoped for forgiveness, for understanding, but instead, he received a painful dose of truth.

Uncle Jimmy looked away, his gaze distant, lost in memories of bygone days. "I can't change the will, Padraig. It's already set in stone. But I can offer you advice. You know, Padraig, there are four main ways of ruining yourself in life," he began. "There's the land and then there's the women - certain type of women that is. And then there's gambling and drinking. The land is the quickest and the least enjoyable. It demands arduous work, pumping every shilling back into it for extraordinarily little return. Women have good qualities, but one must master one's enthusiasm while holding the reins of reason in both hands when holding court with them. And the flighty ones can smell the free-flowing booze from the amadán at the bar from an almighty distance. A fool like you can squander his livelihood away in the blink of an eye abusing all four."

Padraig gulped and his mouth dropped open.

"For I think you've fallen victim to all of these vices," continued his uncle.

Realising his uncle knew more about his affairs than he thought, Padraig's head began to spin. His plan had failed completely. He was at a loss about what to do next. Down, defeated, and desperate, he made one last effort, asking his uncle if he could call again to see him.

"You can indeed. If you look for help and reform your ways."

"What?" whispered Padraig in disbelief.

"I'm an old man, but I'm no fool, Padraig. I believe in the principle that if a person once tells you a lie, then you've put an end to the truth from them forever.

It was a barefaced stunt to show me another man's acres thinking you could pull the wool over an old man's eyes. Good luck to you now, Padraig. But take heed of my words before you end up in here, or worse still in the poor house with a great burden on the state to support you."

Padraig suddenly felt defiant. "You're wronging me. I spent the best part of my life minding my mother, and not one of her own siblings gave a hand, you included, and you with neither chick nor child to mind."

"And for that you were well rewarded, Padraig. With a fine farm where my brother worked like a slave all his life. And now to see it squandered so breaks my heart."

"But I've neither companion nor friends. What else could I do?"

"You became easy prey to bad habits. You spent all your time in the pub and bookies. You shacked up with women who bled you dry, and now the money's gone. And they're gone too. Drinking, smoking, gambling has left you without strength or purpose. Not only have you degraded yourself, but you've also degraded the entire family."

"So, you're leaving everything to my sister Sheila

then, one who has plenty of money already?"

"She has plenty because she minded it, Padraig, and she's married to a good man, Donnie, who won't squander a penny. They're a credit. And there's never a week they don't visit me here."

An uncomfortable silence followed as the truth of his uncle's words took root. Christ, how could he have sunk so low? And to make matters worse, the matron re-appeared as if from nowhere.

You'll be needing another swig from that bottle, if there's any left, that is," she snapped, pointing her finger at the door.

Outside, feeling miserable, chastened by his uncle's words, Padraig drained the last of the bottle, then sped down the pebbled nursing home driveway, vowing it'd be the last drop he'd ever taste in his life.

***

Over the weeks that followed, Padraig did indeed stop drinking, each day without booze becoming more torturous, the wheezing in his chest unbearable, forcing him to visit his local doctor. Once inside the waiting room, the minutes dragged like hours as beads of sweat formed on his forehead. Seeing sick people all around him, he suddenly felt dizzy, and propping his hand on the wall for support, he headed for the door.

Once outside, the faint breeze coming off the estuary made him feel better. He'd swear he could smell the glorious scent of Guinness from Crowley's Bar wafting towards him. The image of malty sweet porter flowing from the tap ushered him back to his old haunt.

Once inside, drinking like a fool, thoughts of his brother-in-law, Donnie Walsh, inheriting his uncle's wealth felt like an aching tooth. His resolve to fix the situation grew as each sip of alcohol triggered his hatred.

"Fucking Donnie Walsh inheriting what's mine," he muttered. "As if the whore hasn't enough already with his Garda pension and his house all paid for. Over my dead body will he or my sister rob me of my entitlement!"

Rummaging through his pockets, finding the last few coins, he stumbled to a nearby telephone box and dialled his sister's number. Sheila answered.

"Put that bollix of a husband of yours onto the phone will you?" Padraig demanded, his words slurred.

"I will not. You're drunk again, Padraig. And Donnie's not home. He's gone to the Galway races. He won't be back for a few days. What do you want him for anyhow?"

Slamming the phone down without answering her question but wanting revenge on his sister for badmouthing him to Uncle Jimmy, Padraig straightened himself, wondering how in the name of God he could get a lift to Galway.

Shuffling from foot to foot to stay warm, paying no attention to the bitter rain thundering down on him, he hitched his thumb in the air for a lift to Galway, singing his favourite song.

I'm not ready to roll over,

I'm still the daddy of them all,

I'm still the top Banana,

They still answer when I call.

I'm older, yes, but I'm wiser,

And they better not forget,

I'm not ready to roll over,

'Cos there's life in the old dog yet.

(Phil Coulter)

As Padraig Moriarity hummed the refrain, 'there's

life in the old dog yet', while hitching a lift to the Galway Races, he couldn't shake off the thrill of anticipation in the air. The longing to languish in the camaraderie and vibrant energy from gambling enlivened his spirit. But most of all, he envisioned the thrill of meeting his brother-in-law, Donie Walsh, and quietly relished the thought of outsmarting him at the races—a subtle yet satisfying chance to set the record straight and turn the tables.

Savouring Secrets

Agnes Smith was distracted.

It had been seven hours since she'd mixed the rat poison through the gravy granules before pouring the thick brown liquid over the roast beef dinner. She was sure her mother should be dying and asking her to be by her side.

But that was not the case.

Retrieving the leaflet from the bin, Agnes re-read the instructions on how to effectively administer rat poison. She feared the unthinkable. What if it hadn't worked? What if her mother hadn't eaten enough gravy to die and instead it had left her with even more debilitating ailments? Suddenly the implications of what she had done, or hadn't done, were so disturbing she stopped reading and closed the pamphlet.

The night dragged on like an ache.

Having worn her rosary beads almost threadbare from beseeching God to let her mother slip away quietly, fear over what a doctor's examination could possibly reveal began to haunt her.

Suddenly, Agnes found herself in a surreal moment. She stood there, paralysed, her eyes locked on her mother, lying in bed, seemingly lost in her thoughts. Then, as if struck by a bolt of realisation, her mother sat up abruptly, a look of utmost urgency in her eyes. With a long, loud gasp, she fell back onto her pillow, almost as if a heavy blow had landed on her head.

Agnes felt time slow down as she waited, her heart pounding in her chest. She knew that this moment could be her mother's last breath. She waited, minutes stretching into hours, unwilling to tear her eyes away, yet afraid to approach too closely.

The silence was only disturbed by the occasional creak of the floorboards and the ticking of a nearby clock.

An hour later, as the realisation sank in that her mother might have taken her final breath, a peculiar silence enveloped the room. Her emotions tangled in a web of uncertainty and grief. She felt her own heart heavy with sorrow.

Finally, Agnes gathered her courage and raced downstairs. Her breath came in hurried gasps as she dialled the doctor's number and then the priest's. She knew the gravity of the situation, and her words were a mix of urgency and distress as she called for their immediate assistance.

"She fought the brave fight," said the doctor,

expressing his condolences after arriving quickly from his Limerick practice in Castleconnell.

Feigning grief, fake tears in her eyes, Agnes replied, "She lived to a ripe old age. I doubt I'll see so many years."

Desperate for release from her predicament as her mother's long-term carer, Agnes smelled freedom. Aged forty-five the following month, she'd believed her chances of marriage were over until she heard John Ryan's engagement had ended, with his fiancé flinging the ring back in his face. Rumour spread in the local pub that he had cheated on her. Hearing the news, her heart had skipped a beat, sensing that she might be able to renew her long relationship with John now that the shackles of her freedom had finally been removed.

She considered herself a formidable catch for any man, her allure heightened by the vast expanse of one hundred and eighty acres of lush acreage in Annacotty. The surrounding rolling hills, adorned with emerald-green grass, embraced her property, providing an enchanting backdrop to her aspirations.

She mused upon the expansive beauty surrounding her. Annacotty nestled gracefully within the county, a picturesque sanctuary wrapped in rolling emerald hills and boundless fields. The tranquil flow of the river

Shannon, meandering gently, added an aura of peacefulness to the location. As the sun descended, painting the landscape in a warm golden glow, Annacotty transformed into a haven of serene beauty. The distant calls of seabirds filled the air, a gentle reminder of the nearby Wild Atlantic Way where Limerick's rugged coastal splendour met the vast expanse of the Atlantic Ocean. Here, the whispers carried by the winds bore stories of the past, present, and the yet-to-unfold future.

The way Agnes saw it, her mother was going to die sooner or later, but it had taken a very long time. Too long! Like a slow gathering storm, the years ebbed by, until Agnes had finally had enough. The struggle inside her became intense, the hatred running through her unbearable. Her mother's taunts and mockery only exacerbated the situation. It was only when a mischievous rat had invaded the kitchen cupboard that the idea came to her. It was a desperate move, but as she saw it, she could help her mother shorten her misery. No one would suspect anything sinister as her mother was ninety-two years old. And if such a small amount of rat poison could kill a rat, sure there was no point in letting the entire tin go to waste. Not when she could put it to such good use.

Later, her arm felt numb from the barrage of

mourners' handshakes, eager to express their condolences after the funeral service.

"Sorry for your troubles, Agnes."

"She'll go straight to heaven, if anyone does."

"She had a heart of gold, that woman."

"Ah sure, I knew Mary all her life. Powerful worker. She transformed the place with the force of her labour. Her contribution to the making of this place was a gift. A pure gift."

Following the solemn funeral mass, neighbours congregated at the house for tea and sandwiches. Amidst the murmuring voices and clinking teacups, Agnes felt an inexorable drain on her spirit. Suppressed yawns parched her throat, and ceaseless scurrying from room to room left her legs sore. Refilling drinks seemed the most mundane task, yet it had her teetering on the edge of exhaustion. As she listened to the endless reminiscences praising her mother's virtuous deeds, it was particularly taxing. The relentless barrier that had always separated them, a barrier she yearned to cross but that her mother resolutely maintained, was the most poignant source of her sorrow.

She longed for the mourners to depart, but they continued to extol her mother's slavish work ethic, kindness to neighbours in times of need, infamous culinary skills, and relentless farm work after her husband's untimely death. While neighbours occasionally wept, for Agnes, emotions were either black or white, and the white was smudged by resentment. She couldn't mourn. Her feelings knotted themselves too tightly together.

All the praise clashed with Agnes' memories of the daily torment she'd endured caring for her mother. The mourners were oblivious to how miserable her life had been. She had coped with a multitude of daily ailments, administering medication for various complaints and enduring the stench of the bedpan. They didn't know about her mother's constant need for attention, coupled with an acerbic tongue that disheartened even the most loving caregivers. She had grown accustomed to dealing with a wide assortment of daily ailments, bunions, corns, swollen ankles, fallen arches, high blood pressure, arthritis, hourly doses of medication, cough mixtures, and potions. Her mother could start a fight over minor issues like milk portions or the consistency of gravy.

Unbeknownst to the attendees, her mother's refusal to accept a coveted bed in a local nursing home had forced Agnes to abandon her beloved teaching job at the local national school. She had worked tirelessly to secure the vacancy but was left embarrassed and red-faced when her mother declined. Being the only child, Agnes was compelled to stay home as the caretaker.

"It's my entitlement," her mother asserted. "And no daughter of mine will pawn me off to a nursing home."

Her mother's assurances that it wouldn't be long before her departure from this world proved futile. Much to Agnes' dismay, her mother lingered for eight long years, during which Agnes shouldered the increasingly burdensome weight of caring for her, enduring her growing selfishness and heightened cantankerous nature.

Lost in her thoughts, Agnes was abruptly pulled back to the present and the throng of mourners. "Did you hear about John Ryan? Heading off to America," announced Una Fitzpatrick, finishing the last of the egg salad sandwiches. Agnes wished she could vanish as Una continued, "You were quite friendly with him, weren't you, Agnes? Walking you home after school and all. Must be quite a shock for you. Maybe you were the other woman? Anyway, they say he's planning on travelling to America."

Her forehead moist with sweat, cheeks flushed, and hands trembling as the cups rattled on their saucer, Agnes replied, "Oh, I knew that," Agnes lied, hurriedly gathering cups and escaping to the kitchen, hoping her nervous demeanour hadn't been too conspicuous.

As the last guest departed, the house finally regained its quietude. Agnes confronted the remnants of the gathering: soiled cutlery awaited collection, crumbs dotted the sitting room, and napkins lay scattered on the carpet. With a tired sigh, she headed upstairs toward her bedroom.

Upon reaching the top of the landing, her eyes fell on her mother's slippers outside her bedroom, triggering a sudden wave of grief. Tears welled up, sorrow washing over her. Had all her efforts to free herself for John Ryan been in vain? Why was he heading to America when she was here, patiently waiting? Hadn't they agreed, during conversations shared secretly, that their lifelong companionship was inevitable? Yet, he hadn't even come to offer condolences. Surely, he owed her that small courtesy before his departure.

Breathless loneliness pressed down upon her. She straightened the eiderdown on her bed and fluffed the pillows before slipping into an exhausted slumber. Her sleep was so deep that she didn't immediately hear the noise—an insistent doorbell ringing. Irritated by the interruption, she stumbled downstairs, hopeful it might be John Ryan finally visiting. Had he decided to come to see her? Perhaps even declare his love?

Upon opening the door, Agnes was met with disappointment. A stranger, a man of uncertain age with a broad smile, stood before her.

"I'm really sorry for disturbing you, but I've come to pay my respects," he said. "I'm Michael Francis McCabe. I apologise for the late hour, but I couldn't make the funeral on time."

Perplexed by his unexpected appearance and still feeling fatigued, Agnes found herself grappling with the disorder in the sitting room. Unable to welcome him amidst the chaos yet hesitant to leave him standing outside, she swiftly decided to usher him into the kitchen. He expressed gratitude and followed her inside. However, it didn't take long for his uneasiness to surface.

"I'm afraid I've some news that may come as a shock to you," the stranger said, his discomfort palpable.

Agnes narrowed her eyes, intrigued. "Go on."

"I really don't know where to start," he continued.

"I'm really tired. So please ..."

"Did your mother ever tell you about her time in England?" the stranger asked.

"Never. My mother was never in England," replied Agnes firmly.

"In fact, she was," the man insisted, kindly meeting her gaze. "She kept it secret throughout her entire life."

Indignant, Agnes stood up abruptly. "That's absurd! My mother wouldn't lie to me about something so significant."

"How do you know?" the man gently countered. "Your mother moved to London as she had relatives there, the O'Rourke family. She met a young man there and fell in love."

Agnes scoffed, her voice trembling with disbelief. "You must be confused or mistaken. The woman you speak of is not my mother." As she turned toward the door, she said, "Maybe it's time you should leave."

"No, please," the man implored. "Just hear me out."

Agnes hesitated, feeling torn between her safe haven and the uncertainty this stranger brought.

"Okay, go on," she relented. "But make it quick. I've no time for baseless tales."

After the man's revelation, Agnes was left in shock. She hesitated between disbelief and a profound curiosity that urged her to listen further. The man, sitting still, recounted his story with unwavering composure, explaining how her mother, Mary, having travelled to England for work, had left two years later under harrowing circumstances.

"Your mother was too young and vulnerable in England at that time," he spoke softly. "Those were desperate days. The Irish faced harsh treatment, discrimination, and disrespect. Your mother was working in a grand house with intolerable conditions. Being Irish meant being ostracised, denied the simplest courtesies. And when her partner left and her baby was only three months old, she couldn't bear the hardship. Distraught and destitute, she relinquished her child and returned to Ireland, leaving as she had arrived, pretending her child had never existed."

Agnes, reeling from the revelations, struggled to accept this tale. "But why tell me now? And why should I believe any of this?"

The man explained, "I am that child she gave up, Agnes."

Agnes was speechless. Emotions surged within her; disbelief mingled with a growing realisation. The man continued to explain how he and his adopted mother had shared clandestine meetings with her mother during Agnes' summer vacations in Connemara, their relationship kept secret to avoid societal judgment and stigma.

"I'm confused. How did you stay connected?"

"Your confusion is understandable. Let me clarify," the man began. "While she worked at the big house, she met a woman eager to adopt a baby. They arranged to correspond and meet yearly if our mother signed an agreement. Jean McCabe, my adopted mother who has since passed away, visited Ireland every summer. They agreed to keep in touch by letter. That's why we always met in Connemara, far away from prying eyes."

"But I was there the whole time. I spent my holidays in Connemara," Agnes protested.

"You did, but we met discreetly in the church," he revealed, touching a bundle of letters from the inside pocket of his coat —letters from her mother—now laid out on the table. Instantly, she recognised the handwriting.

Agnes felt overwhelmed, inundated by memories of her mother's secretive letter-writing rituals. It all came rushing back: the hours her mother spent secluded in her room, the carefully composed letters, and the quiet walks to the post office to mail them. Suddenly, it clicked—the puzzle pieces fell into place, and a wave of clarity washed over her. Tears welled in her eyes as a flood of memories resurfaced.

"You're my brother," Agnes whispered. Her heart

stirred by the thought of having a sibling.

As they conversed, Agnes learned about her mother's pride in her achievements as a teacher, her worries about being a burden, and the untold stories of suppressed love and affection. The brother she never knew she had offered an unexpected sense of belonging.

"Why didn't she tell me any of this?" Agnes wondered aloud.

"It's complicated, you see. Sometimes, certain events are so painful that people find it hard to talk about them. Your mother carried that weight with her for a very long time. Perhaps she didn't want to burden you or disrupt the life she built. Sometimes, keeping silent about such things feels easier than revealing the truth, especially when they're from a past that's very difficult to revisit," he explained.

"Then you must stay," Agnes urged, feeling a sudden rush of protective affection for her newfound brother. "Together, we'll reclaim the land that's been neglected. With your presence, no one will dare claim it for grazing their herd."

As they discussed their future, they agreed to maintain the secret, respecting their mother's wishes. Though questions might arise, Agnes felt elated by the prospect of having a brother by her side.

That night, climbing the stairs after a day filled with anguish and revelations, Agnes felt an inexplicable sense of security. She whispered a silent prayer, thanking her mother for the fortuitous gift of a brother and the promise of companionship and support. In her heart, she felt she was not alone anymore.

***

The days that followed were filled with a peculiar mix of emotions for Agnes. The revelation of her newfound brother, Michael Francis McCabe, had redefined her understanding of her mother and reshaped her own past. Despite the overwhelming revelation, a lingering sense of secrecy clung to their newfound bond.

Agnes and Francis talked incessantly, exploring the nuances of their shared past through the letters their mother meticulously crafted. They found solace in each other's company, discovering shared interests and childhood anecdotes that bridged the gap of years unknown.

As their bond grew stronger, so did Agnes' resolve to maintain their secret. Yet, the ever-watchful eyes of the small village seemed to sense an unfamiliar presence, whispering and gossiping about the peculiar visitor Agnes harboured. But she didn't falter; her newfound boldness shielded their truth, allowing the village to speculate as they wished.

Francis became a familiar figure around the house, tending to the land that had long been neglected. With each passing day, under his caring hands, he slowly transformed the land into a semblance of its former glory.

Their shared secret became a bond they protected, an unspoken agreement to honour their mother's memory and respect her silent plea for concealment. Agnes basked in the newfound feeling of protection and support from her brother, a warmth that filled the void she had unknowingly carried for years.

Through their clandestine existence, Agnes found a liberation she hadn't known before. The prospect of facing the world with a secret made her feel invincible. In her heart, she knew that Francis' presence wasn't just a coincidence; her prince had come to rescue her at last.

As the seasons changed, so did the bond between Agnes and Francis. They shared laughter, tears, and the profound understanding that their unusual situation was a testament to love, loss, and resilience.

Walking side by side to Mass, the curious eyes of the villagers followed, their tongues wagging with questions. Agnes held her head high, embracing the enigma surrounding her and Francis.

But one big secret continued to haunt Agnes. Until she couldn't keep it inside any longer.

"Francis, I need to tell you something," she said one night, finding the courage from a stiff Jameson. "I may be to blame for our mother's death."

"Stop tormenting yourself, Agnes. You gave up the best years of your life to look after our mother. From what you've been telling me, it's clear you made great sacrifices, received little thanks, and suffered a lot of ridicule for your trouble."

"But …"

"But nothing, Agnes. Now let's talk about something else. Something happier. You've been through a very tough situation, and I'd like to make it up to you. I should have been here to share your burden. I also feel guilt. But we can't live in the past."

While Francis talked on, releasing years of unleashed feelings about the mother he knew little about, Agnes listened. She nodded and tried to hide the sadness welling up inside her for him. Wondering how her mother could have denied her son's presence in her life, given that she adored him so much, yet sacrificed that love in fear of evil gossip. How could she tell him?

How could she tell Francis that she had murdered his mother in pursuit of her own freedom? Yet she was unable to contain her secret under a blur of alcohol.

Francis initially dismiss her confession due to her emotional state and the large amount of alcohol consumed. However, she insisted on telling him every detail about how she had used the rat poison, leaving him somewhat suspicious, deciding the story wasn't entirely implausible. It struck Francis that her tears weren't solely for her mother's departure but for the relinquishment of her youth, consumed by the burden of caretaking.

The following morning, Agnes awoke to the inviting aroma of toast wafting from the kitchen. The presence of the newcomer brought a surge of joy that left her heart aflutter. Here was someone remarkable, joyfully preparing breakfast for her. Francis possessed a certain gallantry with deep blue eyes and dark, greying curls, which hinted at a heritage different from Agnes' green eyes and thinning auburn hair. He exuded charm, a capable worker on the farm, unafraid of any task, no matter how challenging.

Agnes found herself captivated by his versatility, marvelling at his ability to mend a dilapidated tractor, harvest hay, and tirelessly cultivate the fields. His profound connection with nature and the land seemed innate, as if he had spent a lifetime devoted to this glorious farm. She observed him like a fascinating puzzle, pondering over how a man who had once worked on English building sites could possess such an inherent knack for farming. As months passed, she regarded his transformation as nothing short of miraculous.

Each morning after enjoying delicious home-made scones and strawberry jam, Agnes would witness Francis bounding into the fields with the enthusiasm of a young calf exploring its surroundings for the first time. She began to believe that, together, they could ascend into a realm of settled contentment, a place she had never ventured before. For the first time, Agnes found solace in a life that flowed smoothly, basking in a newfound happiness that she hadn't previously experienced. She no longer cared for the absent John Ryan, not even for his lack of condolences. There was another man in her life now, a man who brought forth a new love and a sense of security she hadn't known before.

Suddenly, over a game of cards one night, Francis announced that he had to return to England to tidy up his affairs as he had left them unfinished in his hurry to get to the funeral. Shocked by the announcement,

Agnes felt lost again, believing he might disappear forever.

"Can I come with you, Francis? Wouldn't it be wonderful to ..." Agnes began.

"No," he replied, interrupting her before she could finish her sentence. "It's best if I travel alone."

Francis knew he had to leave. For several weeks, he'd been consumed by worry, fearing that Agnes had developed romantic feelings for him like an infatuated schoolgirl. He had initially denied it, but the night they'd shared a bottle of Jameson while drowning their sorrows, Agnes had kissed him gently on the cheek, wishing him goodnight before retiring to her room.

The next morning, he awoke to her caring for him in his bedroom, tending to his hangover with a cool, damp facecloth on his forehead. Doubt crept into his mind, but he pushed it away. On another occasion, he had held her hand with a gentle touch, brought on by their shared grief and too much alcohol. Then, when she'd taken his hand and invited him to dance in the kitchen to Jim Reeves' record 'Put Your Sweet Lips Closer to the Phone', his suspicions were confirmed. As the music played, she paused, looked into his eyes, and she drew him closer during their dance. He felt her warmth, but he gently pushed her away, placing both hands on her shoulders to create some distance. He could see the disappointment in her eyes.

Agnes sat at the kitchen table the next day, gazing out of the window at the scenic Fairy Woods beyond the banks of the river Shannon. Her mind was blank, not knowing how to address her new love, aware that her actions were irreversible. They avoided each other that day, like two strangers entangled in an icy conundrum.

The following morning, she set the breakfast table with fried bacon and eggs and a freshly baked loaf of brown bread. She knew he wouldn't be able to resist the smells wafting through the kitchen. Yet, when he came downstairs, he barely touched his breakfast and sat in silence, brooding and mindlessly pushing crumbs around his breakfast plate.

"Agnes, this isn't the way things should be," Francis finally broke the silence. "We won't find happiness like this."

Although she knew he was right, her feelings had developed too far to be easily quenched.

"So, what should I do now? Remain unloved, unmarried?"

Francis sat there, torn between sparing his sister's

feelings and ending their inappropriate relationship as swiftly as possible.

"The reason is quite simple," he explained. "We are siblings. We can't be together in the way you desire … the way we might want. It's not right."

"We have different fathers. It's not unheard of, and it's not as if I want to get pregnant."

"You're not thinking clearly. You need time to grieve. My sudden arrival and dealing with recent events have overwhelmed you," he said.

"Grieve? More like relief …"

"Stop. This is an unhealthy conversation. I need some fresh air. I'm going for a walk."

"Francis, please … I'm sorry. Let's start over, pretend this never happened."

"You know I can't do that. We can't undo what we've done. My flight is tomorrow. I'll leave you my address in case of an emergency."

As he left the following morning, Francis knew Agnes' spirit would be wounded, but he hoped that one day she would understand that his departure was the right thing to do. Disheartened, he grabbed his suitcase and stepped out into the pouring rain, pondering how the dream of returning to his mother's childhood home had been snatched away as quickly as it had come. He felt guided by his mother's spectral hand, urging him back down the driveway and into his former life.

***

After much contemplation, Agnes finally gathered her thoughts and committed them to paper, writing a letter to Francis.

14/8/1979

Dear Francis,

I pen these words with a heart heavy with regret, fearing I may never lay eyes on you again. The weight of guilt and sorrow engulfs me, knowing that my actions drove you away. Francis, I must confess that I have made a grievous mistake, one that will haunt my conscience for eternity. It's as if I've been starved of affection throughout my life, and when you extended your brotherly kindness, I misunderstood it for something entirely different – something I had yearned for but never truly experienced: the affection and kindness of another man.

Please, dear brother, return home and share the farm with me. It is as much yours as it is mine, even more so because the veil of secrecy that enveloped us deprived you of your rightful place in our family. The silence and concealment robbed us of the chance to grow and bond as siblings should.

I implore you, Francis, to come back. I bear the weight of my wrongdoing and the shame that it brought upon us. Until I know that you can forgive me, I'll carry this burden in my heart.

Agnes

***

20/9/1981

Dear Agnes,

Your letter reached me as I was preparing for work, and it brought me joy to hear from you. I hold no grudge against you, dear sister.

Upon my return, fate led me to meet a remarkable lady at the Crown Pub in Cricklewood. Her name is Mary Harkin, a woman from Sligo, the same age as me. It was a chance encounter while I was lost in thought over a pint of Guinness. Meeting you, feeling the warmth of our embrace, stirred emotions within me that I thought long dormant. The longing for companionship and love coursed through me like a forgotten melody suddenly reawakened.

I share this with you, Agnes, hoping that you too will find love in a similar way. I've chosen to stay here and explore the depths of this budding relationship with Mary. If fate allows, and if Mary reciprocates my feelings, I hope to marry her. May the happiness that has found me someday find its way to you. You deserve the same blessing in your life.

With sincerity, Francis

***

15/3/1982

My dearest Francis,

I was elated to receive your joyful news about meeting a girl from Sligo. The realisation that our chance meeting stirred profound feelings in your heart relieves me of the shame I once carried. It feels as though fate intervened, casting the die and forging a beautiful bond. To think that I played a small p art in it leaves me holding my head high once more. Sadly, my news isn't as uplifting. An old flame of mine, John Ryan, met with a terrible accident on his way to the United States. His hopeful journey toward a brighter future was shattered, leaving him paralysed. I find myself enduring the judgmental glances from neighbours as I step into care for him out of a sense of compassion and shared history. Though I am content with this arrangement, as John and I were childhood sweethearts, I cannot shake off the shadows of those who silently scrutinize my life.

Come home, Francis, with your Sligo sweetheart. The farm is rightfully yours. It holds little value to me and feels burdensome to protect from wandering creatures and covetous neighbours. Let us reclaim the closeness we once shared as a family. Just the four of us.

Agnes

***

As time passed, Agnes grappled with the overwhelming burden of caring for John. She became increasingly exhausted, her spirit worn down, and she began to resent the misfortune that had befallen her once again. Her dreams of lifelong happiness and desires had been stifled by responsibility. Frustration would often boil over into fits of rage, where she'd unleash her anger over even the smallest of tasks demanded of her. Life had lost its meaning, and she questioned why her prince hadn't come to rescue her. The fairytale she'd once believed in now felt like a cruel joke. Ten years in the castle, ten years of being trapped, ten years of longing, and there was still no sign of her prince.

The relentless daily torment forced Agnes into contemplating a sinister way out, and her thoughts turned to the rat poison. It had worked once before, so why not again? In their earlier days, during the bloom of young love, John had been a virtuous man. She could still feel the rush of that first love, but it had withered over the years, leaving John lifeless and in need of constant care, much like her own mother.

The second time around, lacing John's gravy with poison felt easier.

***

January 14, 1984

Dear Agnes,

I will be home for St. Patrick's Day. Mary fell ill and died last year.

Francis

Agnes smiled as she read the postcard. Finally, her prince was coming for her.

***

When the door swung open, the aged look on Francis' face shocked her. He was the same Francis who had once held her close and danced with her in the kitchen, but the wrinkles and the weight of years had taken their toll. His eyes still held their beauty, even in the sharp winter light, but his tired expression couldn't diminish the fondness she felt for him.

"Agnes, my dearest, you haven't changed at all. It's great to see you," he said, as if reading her thoughts.

"I'm so happy you're home, Francis," she replied. "I've your favourite dinner on the range. Come on. You must be famished after that long journey."

"So, where's John? I'm looking forward to meeting him."

"Oh, he had to go into hospital for an operation. Could be there a while. Apparently, there are complications. I"l get you a whiskey."

Francis rubbed the back of his head and looked sheepish. "No whiskey. I'll just put my bag in the scullery to get it out of the way."

As they savoured the hearty roast, Agnes found herself engrossed in Francis' anecdotes about his days working on the London building sites. He appeared relaxed and engaged as they conversed, yet a subtle shift in his demeanour didn't escape her notice. There was an undercurrent of distance, a faint air of reservation that seemed to cloak his usual warmth.

Despite this, she sensed a lingering connection, a hint that perhaps he harboured sentiments for her, unspoken yet present.

"What's the dreadful smell in the yard, Agnes?"

"Oh, that's the neighbour's slurry tank. Dreadful, isn't it?"

"But it wasn't there the last time I visited."

"Depends on which way the wind is blowing. You have a lot to learn yet about farm life," Agnes replied nonchalantly before busying herself, frantically polishing floors.

Over the weeks that followed, a sudden change came over Francis. He abruptly announced that he had an urgent appointment, leaving Agnes with a sense of unease and unanswered questions lingering in her mind. His hasty departure felt out of place, leaving her with a gnawing suspicion that something had altered in their dynamic. The abruptness of his unexplained exits left Agnes feeling disconcerted, as if a door had closed, shutting her out from a part of Francis that had once been open to her.

Every night, as she climbed the stairs to her room, she carried her dreams and desires with her, imagining herself in bed with Francis. In her mind, she was wrapped in his strong, welcoming embrace, her hopes soaring high with possibilities. It felt as though she had awakened from years of slumber into a world of promise.

Yet, the following morning brought a sudden jolt of reality. It had all been a dream—Francis was not there.

Soon, Agnes began to feel unwell. She felt the mounting pressures of time slipping away, a life seemingly bypassed without the chance to experience the fairytale romance she had so long dreamt of. The longing for a 'prince charming' to rescue her from the relentless demands of life intensified, leaving her yearning for a reprieve that seemed elusive. Instead, anger and bitterness began to take hold.

As the days passed, Agnes' emotions swirled. Her desire for Francis remained unquenched, and her thoughts turned to a plan. Then things started to unravel. There was something unsettling in Francis' eyes, something that left her unable to rekindle the illusion of their love. She resented having to try again and again to recreate their past.

One afternoon, out of the blue, Francis asked, "What happened to John?"

"Why do you keep asking about him? He's a ghost. Hovering around my house, our house. He's vaporous, empty as a hologram. He couldn't achieve movement through the mechanisms of his body, so he became a substance lighter than air, then vanished," she replied.

"What a lot of rubbish you're talking," Francis said flatly. "I found his body in the septic tank. I wondered what the smell was for the past weeks. I've had it checked out, Agnes. Did you poison him? Did you do the same to our mother?"

Agnes was gripped by a sudden, chilling sensation creeping up her spine. Abruptly, she began to laugh— hysterically, directly into his face. It was a rapid and startling transformation, akin to flicking a light switch.

"What the devil are you laughing at, Agnes?" he replied aghast.

"You reported me. You traitor. You swine. You deserve to die. Reporting your one true love."

Furious, she careened blindly through the house, flung open doors, toppled ornaments, kicked old newspapers, leaving them fluttering in the air, shattering the speckled mirror hanging over the fireplace. Then with one swift crashing blow, she shattered a table lamp over Francis' head.

Almost instantly, with a sudden, gut-wrenching realisation, she lunged toward him as he crumpled to the floor. She bent over him, her heart pounding. Horror and fear coursed through her veins.

Desperation gripped her as she lowered herself to the floor, pulling him into her lap, cradling his fragile body, his head bloody and battered. With trembling hands, she gently caressed his wounded head.

"Oh, Francis, I only ever wanted to hold you, to love you, and for you to love me back. You were a gift, a new beginning for us both, and now you're a curse."

She waited a long time for her body to recover from its exertions, long enough to drag Francis' body to join John's in the septic tank. Long enough for her to clean up the bungalow, including the blood. Long enough to get dressed and splash water on her face and put on her best coat with its animal collar. Long enough to leave the house with a packed bag to catch the bus to Limerick. Long enough to book into Cruise's Hotel. And long enough to order dinner.

"Roast beef please with all the trimmings."

"No gravy," she insisted.

The Leitrim Atheist

As Ned Muldoon approached Fenagh in the crisp wintry air, the scenic village emerged on the horizon. The serene hush of the wintry season enveloped the landscape, enhancing the essence of the historic village. The distant silhouette of the rolling hills, cloaked in a blanket of snow, stood as silent guardians, preserving the peaceful allure of the Leitrim countryside.

The winding road led him past the hallowed Fenagh Abbey, its ancient stone walls standing as a testament to centuries gone by. The skeletal branches of the trees lining the road reaching skyward were adorned with a delicate dusting of snow, while patches of frost glistened on the lush grass along the roadside. The distant silhouette of the rolling hills stood as silent sentinels guarding the tranquil beauty of the countryside. The soft glow of lights from Quinn's Pub flickered warmly, beckoning him inside, contrasting the wintry chill, promising a welcoming refuge from the cold outside.

Smiling warmly, Ned stood, hands comfortably tucked into his pockets, and tossed a crisp new note onto the well-polished bar counter. He cut an imposing figure, standing close to seven feet tall, wrapped in an immaculate Aran knit jumper, his shirt crisply ironed and shoes gleaming like polished onyx. His pants bore not a single crease out of place, testimony to his meticulous attire. With hair now graced by a touch of silver, reflecting the overhead lights, his eyes sparkled with an earnestness that hinted at both the wisdom of years gone by and the youthful vibrancy that still lingered within him.

Surveying the surroundings like a visiting celebrity, his gaze swept curiously across the gathering in Quinn's Bar. Local musicians picked up a variety of instruments - fiddles, whistles, flutes, a bodhran, and spoons - their melodies effortlessly filling the air. The music triggered memories for Ned, reminding him of the unyielding strength of his dreams. Despite his thirty years in America, the longing for his native Leitrim remained as potent as ever. Recollections of sunlight filtering through the hedgerows, accompanied by birdsong and wildflower meadows, often brought him to tears, reminiscent of an abandoned child yearning for home within the confines of his New York flat.

Despite his time away, his heart remained tethered to the simplicity of rural Ireland—a sentiment alien to those revelling in the lively atmosphere of the pub. Clad in an Aran knit jumper and polished shoes, Ned stood as a stark contrast to the jubilant patrons who had never strayed far beyond their familiar farm gates.

And now, Ned could hardly believe his luck when his homecoming presented a miraculous opportunity - a chance to attend the local Station Mass and perhaps begin to atone for the three decades of his absence from the church while away.

However, it sparked some disapproval among the locals.

"So, after all these years, you're telling me ye're going to confession at the Station Mass in Heeran's," said Tommy Flaherty, scratching his silvery beard and gazing over his pint at the man sitting on the bar stool next to him.

"I am indeed," said Ned. "I'd like to be a cultural catholic this time round, Tommy. Come and go to the sacraments when it suits me."

"How do you think the man above would view that when you meet him at the pearly gates?" Tommy asked.

"Ah, I think he'll be fine with it. This could be my road to Damascus. Except I wouldn't be a believer in all the teachings of Christ's Church like the rest of you practicing Catholics," Ned jibed.

"Sounds like a lazy Catholic to me. You were boasting the other night that you hadn't been to confession or Holy Communion since you left for America thirty years ago. You even said it didn't affect you. Isn't it a momentous change of heart you've had overnight?"

"It might be, Tommy. But the Station Mass might be a handy way for me to start back, don't ye think? The curate will do the confessions while Father McCabe says Mass, and sure he'll be more lenient than the cranky old priest. And he can't waste too much time on me if he wants to plough through the rest of you lot afterwards," Ned beamed.

"Oh, so you're looking for leniency and sacramental absolution from the poor young curate who'll rush through confessions," said Tommy, sipping on his pint, his chubby cheeks redder than normal. "You think he's licensed to let you off scot-free after all these years."

Smiling, Ned shoved his hands deep in his pockets before throwing a twenty-pound note on the bar counter, running a curious eye around the crowd in Quinn's Bar.

His return to the parish of his childhood had brought about this miraculous opportunity for him not only to attend the local Station Mass but to atone, in a most convenient manner, for the three decades he'd abandoned the church.

"Twenty Afton and a Jameson, please Joan and whatever Tommy's having," he said to the woman behind the bar twiddling with a bow in her hair. Her earrings seemed to shine like diamonds, reflecting between the orange flame of the turf fire facing her and the amber glow of the whiskey bottles lining the bar.

"What'll you have, Tommy, a pint or a chaser?" she asked.

"Both, Joan, thank you, and God bless you, Ned."

With his glasses firmly positioned on his nose, Ned breathed in deeply, ruminating upon the advantages of attending Station Mass.

I believe I can be vindicated completely for my sins, Tommy," he said.

"It's bullshit that you need vindication from, Ned," replied Tommy, with a smile, his fulsome stomach straining his checked shirt. "And I should know, with your farm being next to mine."

"Now there's gratitude for a free drink, eh. Isn't it time you bought your own?"

"Don't worry about that, Ned, I'll get the next one. And if it's an oversight of mine, sure, I can always get it wiped off me slate with the big sins."

"Well, isn't that the truth? And isn't that what confessions are all about, Tommy? Cleaning the slate. It's like official forgiveness, rubber stamped by the curate."

"But surely it's a bigger sin, a mortal one indeed, not to have gone to Mass or confession for more than thirty years, Ned?"

"Jesus, Tommy, you're annoying me now. For a Mass-goer, you'd think you'd know the answer to that question."

"I'll have you know, my friend, I try to stay away from any of them sins, mortal or venial."

"Well, for a man who stays away from sinning, it seems strange that you go so often to get your slate cleaned."

"Ongoing renewal for the soul, that's what it is, Ned – same as a car tax. Pay it up and away you go again for another few months."

"Well, haven't I saved myself a fine lot of car tax then, Tommy?"

Silence prevailed while they enjoyed the local band's rendition of *Whiskey in the Jar.*

"Tommy, ye're right," Ned began, his voice carrying a tinge of introspection amidst the lively atmosphere. "I might be searching for a bit of leniency from the young curate, hoping for absolution for my years away from the church. But more than that, I've realised something. The rhythm of these tunes, the warmth of the people, it's a part of me I left behind when I left for these shores to get back to where I was then, if you know what I mean."

Tommy nodded knowingly, his eyes reflecting both understanding and scepticism. "You've been a world away, Ned. It's not easy picking up where you left off after all these years."

"As I see it, Tommy, the Station Mass can't go on too long," said Ned. "With blight in need of spraying before the potato crop fails, those farmers can't afford hanging around. They'll want the job done and the slate cleaned before the smell of Madge Heeran's cooking leaves their mouths salivating."

"By God, Ned, but you've become a fierce, smart one since you left the country with neither an arse in your trousers nor a pair of shoes on your feet."

"Travel broadens the mind," Ned boasted.

"So, you won't be telling the curate everything then, will you? Cos it only makes sense a fella confessing after thirty years would have much more to tell than a regular penitent like me."

Sitting upright on his stool, a steely look in his eyes.

"I'll have you know, Tommy, none of my sins are bad, and also the notion of burning into roasting hot flames for all eternity is a falsehood you've believed in since your First Confession, religion having been battered into you since you were a youngster," he said. "I know the curate's a young man with more intelligence than the old parish priest who believes in all that hell and damnation stuff."

Raising his finger in the air, Tommy was about to interrupt, but Ned kept speaking.

"Sure, can't you see the grief and anxiety that God has inflicted upon poor Father McCabe's face over the years? He's become a tired engine of a man, his face contorted with the strain of his religious teaching. The young curate now hails from a different generation. More intelligent, believing if a man returns to the church in good faith, he's already begun the journey to forgiveness."

Tommy's brow creased, his distress evident as Ned's words jolted his mind back to past experiences from childhood in the confessionnal box. He remembered his fear of the darkness inside as the Redemptorist

Missionary pulled back the shutter and peered through the grille at him, his dark eyes exuding what he thought was vehemence when he'd told him he'd stolen apples from a neighbour's orchard. He couldn't forget how the fear of God was scorched on his mind as the priest warned him he'd rot in hell if he didn't repent for the rest of his life for his evil, premeditated act.

A sudden fear hit Tommy as he remembered how he'd never confessed to laying poison to get rid of the slugs eating his cabbage, but the poison ended up killing the neighbour's dog. Perhaps it was time for him to confess and wipe his own slate clean. Suddenly, Tommy felt large beads of sweat forming on his forehead, memories of the confessional instilling fear that urged him to shift the conversation.

Tommy then announced that he never thought anyone would miss the local area. "Sure, it's the same routine day and night here and the same locals in the bar every night."

Ned sighed, a mix of melancholy and determination etched on his face. "That's true. But I've come to realise that the life I built in America, the hustle and bustle, the towering skyscrapers – it's not where my heart belongs. My soul yearns for the quiet hills, a longing within me for here at home."

The fiddle's haunting melody swept through the bar, weaving emotions that resonated deep within Ned's core. It reminded him of something he'd tried to suppress—a void that no amount of success in the United States could fill. "I've been chasing dreams in the city that never sleeps, but I've lost sight of where I truly belong. It's time to come back to my roots, to find solace in what I've missed the most."

Ned's return to his childhood parish had spurred a change within him, although his previous claims of atheism had left many puzzled, even scornful. As he sat among the familiar faces in Quinn's Bar, nursing his whiskey and engaging in his usual banter with Tommy, it seemed the transition back to his roots had set tongues wagging and eyes rolling.

"An atheist turned devout Catholic overnight, Ned? Now that's a grand old leap," remarked Sean, a local farmer seated across the bar, his scepticism evident in the arch of his brow.

Ned chuckled, the tinkling sound of his laughter echoing across the bar. "Ah, lads, you know me, always one for a bit of jest. Just taking a detour to confession, that's all."

Tommy nodded in agreement, although the expression on his face hinted at cynicism. "Indeed, a

Station Mass to wipe the slate clean. Like a car tax, isn't it, Ned?" he teased, nudging him gently.

Ned couldn't help but smirk. His boasts of being an atheist had always been met with varying reactions, from disbelief to disapproval. Returning to his roots and embracing the faith he'd once abandoned didn't sit well with those who'd listened to his incessant atheist proclamations over the years.

Joan, with a sparkle in her eye, leaned closer to Ned as she wiped the counter. "You're an enigma, Ned Muldoon. One day an atheist and the next back to confession. How do you explain that?"

Ned shrugged, his grin betraying a hint of amusement. "Life's a journey, Joan. Sometimes you find yourself taking an unexpected turn. But don't you worry, I'm just making sure the tracks are all laid straight now."

Sean, sitting in his corner, furrowed his brow. "A convenient change of heart, wouldn't you say, Ned?"

The conversation drifted back to light-hearted banter, yet Ned could sense a subtle undercurrent of disbelief in the air. His return to faith had sowed seeds of doubt among the locals who had once listened to his tales of atheism with a mixture of curiosity and bemusement.

Despite the whispers and questioning looks, Ned felt a sense of peace within himself. His return to the parish, the confession, the Station Mass — it was more than just a religious obligation. It was a reclamation of something he'd left behind a part of himself that had remained tethered to Leitrim, regardless of his absence.

As the lively Irish tunes continued to weave stories within the bar, Ned sat back with a knowing smile. His journey, he realised, was far from over, but for now, the barroom banter and sceptical glances were a small price to pay for finding his way back to what truly mattered.

As Ned and Tommy continued their playful banter, their conversation resonated with the amicable bickering characteristic of old friends who knew each other's quirks inside and out. Joan, the barmaid, expertly multitasked, serving drinks with a warm smile while occasionally interjecting in their lively exchange.

Ned sipped his drink and cast a discerning gaze over the bar, taking in the familiar faces, the crackling warmth of the fire, and the essence of the place that had always felt like home.

Tommy, whose occasional dips into the confessional were a stark contrast to Ned's lengthy absence, playfully continued their verbal jousting. "Maybe you should've considered buying a confessional ticket, Ned? A bulk deal could've saved you quite the fortune on your overdue taxes!"

"Ah, Tommy, give over now about confessions!" Ned chuckled, enjoying the banter.

With a decisive nod, Ned bid farewell to Tommy, leaving the pub with a newfound determination. The Station Mass awaited him—an opportunity not just for confession but a turning point in reclaiming a part of himself he had abandoned long ago. Pondering Ned's words, Tommy thought how wholly typical it was of Ned Muldoon to be able to talk his way out of anything. A lumbering lump of a man, he was by no means a fool. With such determined effort and mind-blowing logic, there was no question, but absolution was in store for him, entitled by the admission of his own superiority on all matters.

On the morning of Heeran's Station Mass, as laughter echoed through the room, Ned and Tommy shared a conspiratorial wink, relishing the satisfaction of their successful confessional stint. Their boisterous demeanour seemed irreverent to some, but to them, it was the glee of having outsmarted the system while still fulfilling their religious duties.

Ned's satisfaction radiated from his beaming face,

and he couldn't help but feel a sense of triumph, having navigated through his confession without revealing the deeper recesses of his past. For him, the confession became a mere formality, a ritual to follow.

The two men's laughter, although drawing disapproving glances from the more devout attendees, seemed to bring a peculiar comfort to others who shared their similar sentiments about the rigidity of religious practices.

After Mass and a hearty feed of succulent glazed hams, home-baked fruit cakes, steaming scalloped potatoes, aromatic roast beef, and an array of freshly baked bread, the congregation gathered in communal spirits to share the sumptuous spread. Later, as the rest of the congregation gradually dispersed, Ned and Tommy chose to linger, fostering a serene and companionable silence between them.

"What penance did you get, Ned?"

"A decade of the rosary. And you?"

"Three Hail Mary's."

With hearts light and spirits uplifted, the two old friends departed, each contemplating the nuances of faith, absolution, and the idiosyncrasies of religious customs in a world that often demanded strict adherence but seldom left room for personal interpretation.

***

As the weeks passed, Ned and Tommy found themselves unintentionally evolving into local figures whose escapade at the Station Mass continued to be a subject of intrigue and contemplation.

Their mischief became a catalyst for ongoing dialogues among the locals about the significance of confession, the nature of repentance, and the validity of personal interpretations within religious traditions.

Ned, the self-proclaimed 'cultural Catholic', began to engage in thoughtful discussions with various members of the community. He found himself speaking openly about his journey from staunch atheism to a reconsideration of his relationship with the church. His willingness to discuss his doubts, beliefs, and questions about faith sparked a sense of camaraderie among those who, too, grappled with similar uncertainties.

Tommy, on the other hand, unexpectedly found himself approached by individuals who sought counsel about their own spiritual dilemmas. His reputation for staunch adherence to religious rituals paradoxically made him a source of comfort for those wrestling with doubts and questions about their faith.

Over time, the Station Mass incident evolved into a local legend, sometimes comically referred to as 'The Confession Caper'. It became an anecdote shared in hushed tones among the locals, often leading to hearty chuckles or thoughtful contemplation, depending on the listener's perspective and the amount of alcohol consumed.

As the aftermath of the Confessions Caper settled, Ned and Tommy found themselves inadvertently becoming the subject of both amusement and contemplation among the locals. Their escapade had taken on a life of its own, becoming the go-to topic for jovial banter and storytelling in Quinn's Bar.

Each evening, as the dimly lit pub filled with familiar faces seeking solace and camaraderie over a pint of stout, Ned and Tommy regaled the patrons with embellished versions of their infamous Confessions Caper.

Perched on their respective stools, surrounded by the comforting warmth of the hearth, they animatedly recounted the tale, each iteration growing more flamboyant and humorous than the last. Their camaraderie and quick-witted banter added to the entertainment.

Their comic performances, infused with local wit and exaggerated storytelling, turned the Confessions Caper into a cherished local legend, their storytelling prowess earning them free rounds of pints and uproarious applause from the appreciative patrons.

Amidst the clinking of glasses in Quinn's Bar and the jovial echoes of laughter, Ned and Tommy, unwittingly, but happily, embraced their roles as entertainers, weaving laughter and camaraderie into the locals — a testament to the enduring power of laughter and the simple joy of storytelling over glorious pints of the black stuff.

Footnote: Station Mass in Ireland

The tradition of the Station Mass dates back to a period when the practice of Catholicism in Ireland was restricted during the Penal Laws (late 17th to early 18th centuries). To sustain their faith, Irish Catholics gathered in secret at the homes of wealthy families who had private chapels to celebrate Mass. After the Penal Laws were lifted, this tradition continued, evolving into a practice where Mass was celebrated at different homes in a parish. The Station Mass became a communal event, with families taking turns hosting it. It fosters a sense of community and devotion, and it's often held on specific feast days or during Lent, enabling parishioners to gather, celebrate Mass, and share in spiritual unity.

Piseogs

Radiant with anticipation, Maura McHale admired her reflection in the mirror, her wild blond curls gathered and swept neatly behind her ears. Dressed in a navy trouser suit and a pristine white blouse from Foxford Woollen Mills, she felt every inch the serious contender for the bank job she'd been eyeing. It was a welcome departure from the monotonous dark green school pinafore and matching cardigan she'd worn for her entire time at the Sacred Heart School in Westport. The letter inviting her for a job interview at the bank had been a source of immense pride for the McHale household, prompting them to spare no expense to ensure their only daughter looked her absolute best.

"Time to hit the road," called her brother John from the back door. "It's a four-hour journey to the city, and finding the Bank of Ireland's headquarters might be a bit of a challenge."

Snatching her black patent handbag from the kitchen table amidst the faint crackle of burning turf in the range, a pang of melancholy gripped Maura as she bid farewell to her mother. Embracing her tightly, she felt the weight of her mother's hollowed cheeks and noticed her hair elegantly secured with a few loops of fine green ribbon, framing her serene, pale eyes.

Just then, Maura's father, Paddy, entered the kitchen, his wide grin concealing a hint of emotional turmoil. It was the first time Maura would leave home without either parent accompanying her. Barely weeks after her eighteenth birthday, she was grappling with a mix of bittersweet emotions. As Paddy offered words of encouragement, attempting to mask his own feelings, Maura caught a glimpse of his trembling lower lip. Suppressing her own tears, she made a silent vow to make her family proud, feeling a wave of both excitement and sorrow for the new chapter that lay ahead.

Stepping outside, Maura inhaled deeply, taking in the familiar Mayo landscape. The rugged, rolling hills, lush and green, extended into the horizon — a picturesque quilt adorned with grazing sheep and sporadic stone walls. The distant cries of seagulls filled the air a gentle reminder of the ever-present Atlantic Ocean nearby.

As Maura walked with her father toward John's car, she noticed the toll that years of work on their forty-acre farm had taken on him. The labour had left him hunched and weathered. In the rear-view mirror, she caught a glimpse of her mother, Kathleen, going through the ritual of sprinkling Holy Water over the car, customary before embarking on a significant journey down the narrow boreen leading to the main road.

Relaxing for the lengthy journey ahead, Maura took in the familiar sights of the old farmyard amidst sprawling fields and wandering livestock. Tractor tracks cut through the fields, some muddied with potholes filled with liquid dung. She quietly resolved that if she secured the bank job, she would help her parents renovate the entire property, hoping to bring comfort to their challenging lives.

Their tranquillity was suddenly interrupted as the car lurched to the side, causing Maura to brace herself against the dashboard.

"Jesus Christ," exclaimed John, forcefully pressing the brakes.

The Ford Anglia screeched to a stop, grazing the side of a donkey that had unexpectedly dashed onto the boreen. The startled animal fled into the adjacent field, leaving Maura gripping the door handle in freight.

"Oh, God above, I hope that's not a bad omen," Maura tentatively remarked, echoing her mother's superstitions.

"No, Maura, don't talk like mother," John reprimanded firmly. "It's just as well she didn't witness this."

"She would've said it's a forewarning about potential misfortune ahead," Maura retorted with concern. Maura knew her mother held traditional superstitions and would surely interpret the appearance of a donkey spooked by the lights of the car as a sign of bad luck.

"Enough of that nonsense," snapped John. "We can't let superstitions control us. It's all rubbish."

Revving the engine, John discarded the notion of signs or warnings as mere superstition, fully prepared to resume the journey.

As the journey to Dublin unfolded, the whispers of superstitions lingered in the air, amidst the backdrop of rolling green hills and the ever-present sea. She carried both her mother's apprehensions and her family's hopes in her heart as John drove swiftly along the road, eager to make up for lost time.

Driving along the main road to Dublin, with John anxious to make progress after the unexpected delay, Maura noticed an old woman standing at the side of the road dressed in a dark shawl. The mystical mountains loomed in the distance, and a feeling of reverence for nature and the spirits overcame her. The old woman held a holy picture between her two hairy hands, while the silver waters of Lough Mask shimmered nearby.

Staring in disbelief at the apparition before her, Maura recalled seeing the woman once before when she had come to live in a tiny rundown cottage on the neighbouring farm. On that occasion her attention was drawn to the woman's wrinkled hands, adorned with various rings; but one, in particular, caught her eye — an amethyst ring as big as a bishop's, glinted with an inexplicable brilliance. She remembered how the contrast of the radiant gem against the woman's weathered skin sent a shiver down her spine.

Rumours of her eviction and supposed magical abilities had swirled through the community, painting her as someone capable of casting spells.

Suddenly, John forcefully pressed on the accelerator, causing the car to roar loudly and emit plumes of smoke from the exhaust.

"John, what on earth?" Maura exclaimed, her nerves rattled. "You'll lose control. Slow down!"

"Hold on tight," he replied tersely. "I just want to put some distance between us and that supposed witch. They say she's got powers. Better to steer clear and not invite any bad luck upon us."

"God, I thought you didn't believe in superstition!" Maura retorted, exasperated. "Is it not enough to have mother with her superstitions; we don't need you adding to it."

Once they were beyond the old woman's sight, John eased off the accelerator, and Maura couldn't help but feel that perhaps her mother's holy water had played a part in guiding them safely past the enigmatic figure.

With a sense of reassurance settling within her, Maura leaned back, determined not to let a chance encounter with a donkey or any superstitions dampen her hopes for a dream job, far removed from the muddy fields of her native Mayo.

As the miles rolled on, the glorious Nephin mountains faded behind them, making way for Dublin's concrete jungle. The mystical allure of Mayo's landscape gave way to the bustling urban sprawl.

Navigating the labyrinthine streets, John pulled up at the Bank of Ireland's entrance just in time for Maura's interview. Frustrated by the city's congestion and hostile drivers, he circled around, finally spotting a space directly across from the bank.

While waiting for Maura, an odd sensation

overcame John, an inexplicable discomfort lingering at the back of his mind. Dismissing it as city stress, he glanced toward the bank and caught sight of Maura emerging. He called out her name to direct her to where he had parked. Flashing a smile, she raced towards his car.

What followed was a whirlwind in John's mind. He remembered seeing Maura's body tossed like a child's doll onto the bonnet of a passing car, the metallic screech of brakes as traffic came to a jolting stop. It happened in a fraction of a moment yet felt like an eternity. Her figure was flung mid-air before crashing onto the unforgiving asphalt, a scene both surreal and horrifying. The cacophony of surrounding voices, sirens, and screams reverberated through the air, haunting John's senses.

Bolting from the car, he sprinted towards Maura, now motionless on the busy street. His heart clenched in anguish as he pushed people out of his way, desperation surging through him. He wrapped his arms around her, tears streaming down his face as he repeated her name in a frenzied plea. The weight of her body felt surreal, her pulse absent. Panicked and disoriented, he roared at onlookers to call for help, his voice laced with desperation.

Within moments, a police car arrived, followed swiftly by an ambulance. Paramedics rushed to Maura's side, conducting a careful and thorough assessment. John watched in disbelief, his body trembling from shock and anguish, his heart pounding with dread. As he held onto her, praying for her survival, a heavy silence descended upon the chaotic scene. A single glance from the medics left him hollow – a mute acknowledgement that shattered his hopes.

"I'm Garda White," said one of the policemen. "Can everybody please stand back? Who was the driver of the car?"

John's mind was a whirlwind of fear and apprehension. He explained what had happened, the panic rising in his voice. But amidst the turmoil, a sudden realisation struck him—a paralysing truth that he was the cause of the accident. If he hadn't shouted her name, she might not have dashed across the road. He could hardly process it, consumed by a profound sense of guilt and remorse.

As paramedics prepared to transport Maura, John remained motionless, the weight of his actions bearing down on him heavily. The ambulance sped through the thronged streets of Dublin, John clinging to the fading hope of her survival, grappling with the irrevocable consequences of his actions.

John's hands trembled as he found a phone to ring home, his heart pounding with apprehension. The thought of calling home with the devastating news felt like a weight upon his shoulders. Dialling his parents' number, he hoped against hope for some miraculous turn of events.

His mother answered the phone, her voice buoyant with excitement. "John, love, we just got a call from the bank! Maura's interview went splendidly! She got the job! Isn't that wonderful?"

Tears welled in John's eyes, his voice caught in his throat, unable to muster the courage to shatter their joyous news.

"That's ... that's great, Mum," he managed, his voice strained with emotion.

"John, is something the matter? You sound upset," his mother inquired, sensing the unease in his tone.

For a moment, he hesitated, torn between revealing the truth and shielding them from the unsettling reality of what occurred to Maura. How could he break their hearts with the news, especially when they were celebrating such a significant moment for Maura?

"N-nothing, Mum. Just ... just tired from the

journey. I'll call back later," John murmured, his voice cracking as he hung up.

Devastated, John slumped against the hospital wall, choked by a mix of sorrow, guilt, and an overwhelming sense of helplessness. The weight of his silence gnawed at his conscience, yet he couldn't bring himself to shatter their joy. The pain of hiding the truth from his parents was unbearable. So was the thought of having to break the bad news should Maura not survive.

Unable to enter the operating theatre, John wandered along the hospital corridor and later through the city streets to fetch his car. His mind remained fixed on the notion that the old woman had woven a curse, bringing about the tragic incident. As doctors fought to save his sister's life, he sat in his car amidst the hospital parking lot, isolated and desolate, rain pouring down relentlessly outside.

A knock on the window startled him. Through the foggy glass, he recognized Garda White, the officer who had responded to the accident.

"Good evening, sir. You're John McHale, right?"

"Yes, of course. Don't you remember me from the accident?" John replied.

"Accident?"

"Yes, my sister was hit by a car today."

"I'm sorry, sir. I don't recall. But it's a busy day, as you know. And we can all look the same in uniform."

John felt a wave of offense, insisting, "It *was* you … I'm sure …"

"Regardless, your sister Maura contacted us. She's safe, already back home near Westport. She asked us to find you and bring you home."

"That can't be right. Maura was seriously injured. She might be …"

The guard pulled out a notebook and read aloud, "Maura McHale was taken home by ambulance. Contact her brother, John McHale, with the red Ford Anglia car, registration number IT 79682. Urgently come home. The evil witch is dead and buried."

John gasped, a shiver coursing through him.

"Does that message make sense to you, Mr. McHale?" Garda White asked.

"Yes, thank you," replied John, totally confused and shaken by the news.

The supernatural beliefs of his family began to feel more than mere superstitions. The day's harrowing events left him haunted, burdened by unanswered questions, pondering the mystical truths within his heritage.

In the years following, the McHale family lived in a state of profound change, deeply affected by their newfound perception of inexplicable forces within the Mayo landscape—the windswept cliffs, the mysterious caves, and the enigmatic sea, each carrying a tale of spirits that lingered in their lives like shadows in the night.

Footnote: Piseogs in Ireland

Piseogs, originating from the Irish word 'piseog', meaning superstition or omen, are a collection of traditional folk beliefs deeply embedded in Irish rural culture. These customs, spanning various practices and rituals, have been passed down through generations. They include a wide array of beliefs, from avoiding certain actions on specific days to observing rituals to ward off misfortune. Though somewhat fading in modern times, these superstitions have historically influenced daily life, agricultural practices, and local customs in rural Ireland.

Regrettable Dalliance

Kicking his hobnailed boots under the range after returning from Bay View Stores, Sean McGowan placed his daily purchase of Sweet Afton and batch loaf on the kitchen table.

Settling into the warmth cast by the crackling range, he drifted into slumber nestled in the comforting embrace of the armchair. His mind wandered back to beloved Peg, remembering her immense pride when he returned to college in his late fifties. She had never complained about making financial sacrifices on the farm to pay his substantial college fees, only seeing his four-year attendance at Galway University as granting her husband renewed purpose in life.

Sean's time in college saw him become invigorated amidst a cohort of young students, with one sweeping him away. Moya Sullivan was an artist, intense and pretty, who didn't veer into crazy despite being creatively gifted. Taller than him, with an attitude to match her towering height, twenty-five years his junior, she had a thick mane of brown curls flowing to her shoulders and two beautiful brown eyes dancing with devilment. Sean basked in her admiration of what she described as "his brilliant mind".

Smitten by her interest in him, the twinkling tease in her eyes each time they met brought on a surge of lust, leaving Sean with a feeling he'd not expected to have for anyone other than his wife. But he remained sceptical. Such beauty would be waiting for a more deserving suitor than he, one much younger. So simple friendship was as much as he could hope for.

Then one day: "You remind me of my father," Moya said.

Despite his pleasure in her continued interest in him, Sean wasn't entirely flattered by the father-figure comparison. But he was curious.

"In what way, Moya?" he asked.

"Protective."

"Is your father very protective of you then?"

"He was before he died. I was eight years old."

"I'm sorry to hear that. Do you miss him?

"Yes, but you remind me so much of him. In a safe way, of course."

As weeks turned into months, Sean lingered over Moya's every word, eventually believing she was indeed physically attracted to him. Their flirtation grew until one day when they were alone, she crept up on him.

Turning suddenly, the shock causing him to drop his textbooks, Sean felt a blush spread under his collar and burn through his cheeks. Then Moya leaned in and kissed him. Clearing his throat with a mild dry-as-dust cough, a sure sign he was nervous, he kissed her back. That led them to the cloakroom. Driven by desire, Sean succumbed easily.

Such covert encounters continued for weeks. But even though - or maybe because - the erotic pleasure seemed to increase with each one, Sean soon became haunted by guilt, tormented by his betrayal of his beloved Peg who had sacrificed so much for him. At the same time, he remained flattered, in the realisation that he still had the power to attract a beautiful, young woman. Eventually, he convinced himself that his encounters with Moya were harmless. In fact, he even considered the affair might spice things up romantically with Peg, that it had set fire to a passion that had lay dormant but now could be resurrected again. Thinking of Peg in their early years together, he remembered her as a beauty with fierce blue eyes set in porcelain skin, a unique purity about her reminding him of a geisha girl with a sweet and delicate doll's face, white as flour with a tiny rosebud pout that made her look demure. A striking woman, with a figure as narrow as a blade, a Trojan worker, her situation forced upon her as sole heir to her parents' farm.

While Sean's hopes of rekindling their passion were high, sadly - disillusioned by their previous fruitless attempts - Peg showed little interest in participating. Longing for her to be blessed with the legend of Sligo, particularly Queen Maeve's voracious sexual appetite, he resigned in his efforts to entice her. He was clearly no Ailill mac Máta, he reflected, who wallowed in unabashed sexual desires.

Then, sadly, fate intervened.

***

Due to difficulty in reaching him at the university, Peg was already in intensive care when Sean arrived at Sligo General Hospital on the day of the farm accident.

Seeing her motionless under the bed sheets, bruises on her neck and face, tubes and drips feeding liquid and medication through her arm, almost broke his heart into pieces. Nothing had prepared him for the pathetic vision before him. Taking her hand in his, he tried to communicate with her, but Peg simply stared ahead blankly, showing no signs that she even realised anyone was in the room with her. Bending over her bedside, kissing her gently on the forehead, Sean swore to take care of her, to nurse her back to full health.

"Ah, Peg, my darling Peg …" he whispered lovingly as his sense of guilt over his affair mounted madly in his mind.

A doctor appeared. I'm afraid she won't survive an operation. Severe damage caused to her heart has meant her blood circulation is weak. There's a blockage; no blood is getting to her vital organs."

Sean listened wide-eyed, horrified. "Is there nothing you can do? Nothing at all to save her?" he said, his voice pleading.

"I'm afraid we can only make her comfortable," the doctor replied softly.

"Comfortable … is she not comfortable now?"

"She is, but we'll make her even more so. I promise."

"How long can she survive?"

"A few days, maybe. But no longer. I'm so sorry."

Two days later, Peg was dead, without ever responding to Sean's constant presence by her bedside, his gentle touch, or his heartfelt words of love.

Following her burial, the weight of grief on Sean's shoulders, on every part of his body, was exhausting. Unable to excuse himself from her death, he blamed it on his dalliance with a girl half his age, which only served to double his grief and guilt day and night. No matter how hard he tried to blank out his affair with Moya, he failed. It was always there, tormenting him mercilessly. His mind became a prison from which there was no escape, always reminding him of certain incidents where he'd let Peg down. Like the morning she'd asked him to accompany her to the rocky field.

"Sean, I'm going to mow the rushes in the rock field today," she'd said. "Will you come give me a hand? I hate mowing that meadow on my own. The tractor always breaks down in the lower corner beside the rock."

Pausing, remembering a pre-arranged liaison with Moya, he'd replied, "I will, but in the afternoon. I don't want to miss today's lectures." But it was lust not lectures that was on Sean's mind, and he hadn't returned to help her. Moya's needs were urgent, her desire uncontrollable, leaving him unable to resist her.

Night-time was toughest for Sean, alone with clashing thoughts in his mind. Of how he could never hold Peg in his arms again, kiss her tiny forehead, sleep beside her and her pretty and pure figure in her flannel nightdress. But also, of how quickly he'd been overtaken by his animal hunger for Moya. Peg was ten thousand times better in every way than he, and he'd failed her in the most personal of ways any man could ever fail a woman. He would have given all the gold in the world to have her back. To have her fall hopelessly in love with him again. To have her comfort him like when he'd told her the secret from his past, about losing his only sibling in street fighting during The Troubles in Northern Ireland. To have her look into his eyes and tell him he needed, he deserved, a fresh start, a new beginning, with her.

"The time is right for us, Sean. It's a miracle we met," she'd said. She believed in him. Such a simple gift, but so rare and precious. That was why he'd fallen hopelessly in love with her. His thoughts continually transported back to the enjoyable times he'd shared with her and the pleasures they had brought.

Oh, how he longed for the days when they'd once found a love as deep and boundless as the Ox mountains that surrounded them. He believed the mountain's craggy cliffs, cloaked in heather and gorse, bore witness to their love story. It was on one of their first walks, hand in hand, that they'd ventured beneath the towering presence of Benbulbin, their hearts as enchanted as the paths before them. Benbulbin, a silent yet profound witness, cast its long shadow over their shared dreams, sheltering their hearts as they fell hopelessly in love.

Their love drew in the enchanted realms of Sligo, where the rugged beauty of nature merged seamlessly with the whispers of ancient legends. And what he would give to have them back and walk through hills adorned with sheep, through lush valleys and secret glens, whispering sweet nothings and promises of forever. He believed then that their love wasn't just a passing breeze but a force of nature as enduring and profound as the landscape.

Now, in the quiet shadow of her absence, those memories transformed into a bittersweet ache. The memories hurt more than the rocks that held the secret to countless tales, more than the memories themselves; beautiful yet piercing. He would have given gold to have her back.

As time progressed, Sean couldn't help but believe that Peg's death was a form of punishment for his furtive dalliance with Moya. Bouts of depression plagued him, triggered by memories of how he'd ignored Peg's final request to accompany her to the rocky ground she'd dreaded working on alone. After Peg's death, the revulsion and loathing he felt towards Moya unsettled him. Cursing her advances, Sean sought comfort in the fact that he hadn't been the initiator, but neither had he rejected her advances. In truth, he'd taken everything an old man with wrinkling skin and grey hair could take from a beautiful young woman while wallowing in instant gratification.

Haunted by thoughts of Peg and Moya, Sean started drinking, more for escape from reality. One night he became involved in a brawl in his local pub, forcing him to go home to the horrors of a lonely kitchen, where he sat lost, pressing the TV remote in the hopes of finding distraction. Unsuccessful, he thought a few nightcaps might induce sleep. Grabbing the Jameson bottle on the shelf, a bunch of memorial cards came tumbling to the floor. "Damn it," he shouted, picking them up and throwing them on the kitchen table. Then, through a blur of alcohol, his attention was drawn to one envelope addressed to Peg. One he hadn't seen before. Instinctively, he tore it open, wondering how a memorial card could be addressed to Peg!

08/01/1969

My Darling Peg.

I long to tell you how much I cherished our time together last month and how I will count the hours until we meet again. I envision you, sitting in your armchair by the warm hearth, a cup of tea clasped in your hands, two Rich Tea biscuits poised for their comforting dip. Yet, a pang of concern grips my heart, knowing that you might be waiting, alone, perhaps fearing the return of Sean from the pub, lost in the haze of drink.

My feelings for you are the same as when I first noticed you at Grange School. I was dazzled by your beauty then, and still now I cannot resist staring at your photograph with your beautiful blond curls falling around your angelic face. I kiss it nightly and keep it close to my heart before falling asleep. I dream constantly of seeing you and holding you in my arms again.

Oh, Peg, how can you deny yourself the complete happiness we share together each time we meet? The only thing keeping me alive is that our absence is but temporary. I yearn for the day when we can embrace without constraints, where our love can blossom unburdened by the shackles of circumstance.

Forever yours,

Pat

Staring at the letter in disbelief, Sean scrunched the note up tightly in his fist then flung it across the room against the wall.

"Ah, Peg … Peg … what have you done … where's all your religion now, all your church-going and pious nonsense … vows of love and loyalty until death do us part … Jesus, Peg!"

The madness of what he was shouting brought on a wave of misery and a bout of uncontrolled drinking, leaving him sprawled unconscious on the floor.

Next morning, early, it still being dark outside, he was woken by a burst of thunder roaring down the Ox Mountains. Gathering his thoughts, he suddenly remembered the letter. Using the wall as support, he struggled to his feet, steadied himself, and made his way towards the kitchen, the horror of last night's discovery hitting him again like a bolt of lightning. His head thumped and stars danced before his eyes, making him dizzy as he turned on the light and found the letter. Stumbling to an armchair, he re-read it with a sinking heart. Knowing full well what he'd seen, couldn't be unseen.

Every word seemed to bite into his very soul as he read about Pat's longing for Peg and about them being together. He remembered Pat and she had been childhood sweethearts and wondered if Peg had ever really loved him even after they were married. The aching in his heart was unbearable, choking him from the inside out, as he realised his beloved Peg was desired by another man in the same way he had once desired her.

Hours later, his anger abating, a sudden thought unfolded. Peg had experienced that inner churning that made her feel needed, desired by another, someone who loved the purity of her being. But that may not have meant they were in love with each other. Or had they been? Perhaps Peg had experienced something she had not expected to feel again, just like he had felt with Moya. So why should he be angry with her or with himself? In the back of his mind, Sean knew he was seeking a convenient way to forgive himself, but he did feel his unbearable burden of guilt begin to slowly lift, like the mist disappearing over Coney Island.

Later, lighting his Sweet Afton, he buttered the last slice of batch bread, pondering how little he had really known about the person closest to him. Broken-hearted, he contemplated how a pile of secrets had, within a year and without any warning, destroyed them both, leaving an orphaned love affair and an outcast in its wake.

The Bus to Ballybrit

Silence reigned on the bus back from Ireland's biggest annual racing event of the year. Gone was the heavy traffic that had forced it to meander at a snail's pace among horseboxes and trailers headed towards Galway earlier.

Gone was the fun-loving atmosphere of the beer-sozzled revellers eager to flex their wallets and wits on hot tips. Sitting alone, Padraig Moriarity pondered the day's events, wondering how his friends had reacted to the surprise he'd set for them.

***

It had all started in a corner of O'Connell's Bar in Galway's Eyre Square, a hush-hush meeting just before they'd boarded the bus that fateful morning. That was when Moriarity revealed his masterful plan to his brother-in-law and the most unsuspecting bunch of misfits.

"Ye're mad," whispered Sean McGowan upon hearing him. "There's saner people locked in the lunatic asylum."

"Well then, why don't you join them?" snapped Moriarity. "It might be more to your liking to pace back and forth in the grounds of an institution with spits coming out of your mouth like icicles, twirling your rosary beads to kill time. But not me. I'm not ready for extinction yet."

Garda Sergeant Donnie Walsh hadn't uttered a word. Based on his years in the force, he considered his brother-in-law's idea to be borderline madness. Yet, a quiet internal voice spoke to him. His years in the force had brought few thrilling moments in his life. Risk, yes. Danger too. But alongside them there was a wonderful sense of pleasure and satisfaction. Interdependent, like counter forces of a powerful electric current.

The group had formed a bizarre bond in the pub, reigniting the buzz of adventure that previously appeared beyond their reach. Age had crept up like a thief in the night, robbing them of their collective misspent youth. Walsh felt his heartbeat that little bit faster at the prospect of joining this most unlikely bunch of bandits he had ever witnessed in his long working career, with a plan so ridiculous, so hare-brained, so unpredictable that only the minds of mad men under a blaze of alcohol could concoct it. But he also knew that no fraud squad, no team of investigators, would ever suspect such a plan could be created by a bunch of aged men in need of recharging the batteries of their youth. Walsh surveyed his four accomplices with a sudden surge of hunger within him for one last roll of the dice.

"So, what do you bring to the table to pull this off, Bradshaw?" he asked.

"A lot more than you, Walsh, my good man," replied George Bradshaw, sitting across from him.

"Really? And what would that be that's so precious?"

"I served in the British army for thirty years. Learned a lot more tricks of the trade than you lot this side of the water."

Taunted, Walsh felt the voice of British mockery echo in the air.

"And did you ever manage to put yourself in danger of being shot by criminals?" he replied, trying to control his anger. "Like myself, the time they tried to kidnap Shergar, one of the greatest racing-horses ever. Were you ever involved in anything like that, eh … on the far side of the water?"

"That'd be beneath me," sneered Bradshaw. "We rarely competed with the folly of the Irish."

"Is that so? Well, let me tell you, I participated in undercover work, deep inside criminal circles. Got awards within the force for it, too."

The other would-be accomplices soon tired of the one-upmanship.

"By God, with the fine pair of brains between you, isn't there an almighty chance we'll be able to pull off our little swindle?" said Ned Muldoon mockingly. "Sure, it pales into insignificance compared to what you two have experienced in your mighty careers. It's no wonder ye both haven't been canonised by the Pope himself."

"You're right so, Muldoon," laughed Moriarity. "Sure, the boys sound ready to tumble Wall Street itself. If they don't get carried away with their own brilliance, that is."

Silence ensued as each of the men thought about what lay ahead.

Walsh analysed the situation. Compared to the men he had been used to working with in the force, a well-trained backup team with drive and ambition to climb the career ladder, this lot was a bunch of misfits. But their eagerness for the task at hand was not to be underestimated. The prospect of jumping in with them headlong both inspired and excited him. A know-all from Leitrim, Muldoon thought his stint in America had gained him the wisdom and notoriety of a high king. His brother-in-law was a chancer from

Kerry, down and out with nothing to lose, but with a hell of a lot of useful contacts in the racing world and an uncanny ability to pull off a stroke. A widower from Sligo, McGowan dreaded the idea of returning home after his wife's tragic death, while he was having an affair with a student. And Bradshaw, a conceited Englishman, yes, but he was a British army officer after all. That counted for something surely. Hardly the makings of the A team, he thought. But the sheer madness of the idea may just be the key to its success.

Walsh didn't want to think about the implications if things went belly-up, preferring to wave away stray thoughts of how his fellow guards would talk about him in the barracks over mugs of strong tea laced with whiskey, laughing their hearts out for years to come. Another drink would help banish that notion, he thought.

"Another round, Muldoon?" he asked.

"Think it might be your round, Walsh?"

"Not sure it is. Bradshaw, you're slacking a bit. Hope it's not a sign of things to come."

Glaring at him, Bradshaw stood up and made his way to the bar, returning minutes later to bang a pint so forcefully in front of Walsh it splattered both their faces. Walsh beamed. At last, he'd managed to get under his skin. The game was now well and truly on.

"Are you in or out then, Walsh?" asked Moriarity. "We haven't all day, you know. I need to ring Jackie and frighten her away from her betting stall so we can take it over for a few hours."

"And how under God's earth do you think you can frighten off anyone who has just gone to the trouble of getting a license and setting up a stall, ready to make a fortune at the biggest race meeting of the year?"

"Don't you be worrying. Leave Jackie to me. I know her. I've squandered a fortune with her throughout my gambling years. She's ruthless and a charmer to boot, with the power to milk bets out of you with the poorest of odds."

"I'm a bit lost for words here, lads," Bradshaw piped up. "What's a betting stall lady's cunning got to do with us?"

"Ah well, you see, as I said, I know her," rejoined Moriarity. "In the Biblical sense like. I enjoyed many a night in her arms, and pillow talk being what it is, she confided in me that she owes a fortune to the revenue people in overdue taxes. So, I know how to put the frighteners on her."

"For Christ's sake lads, get a grip!" spluttered McGowan suddenly. "We're not going to get involved in anything like that, are we? If so, ye can count me out."

"Hold your nerve, McGowan," said Moriarity. "Calm down. If you don't keep it together, we might as well call it a day."

McGowan did as he was asked, breathing heavily but slowly. Thoughts of himself in an empty house returned to him, the sound of a boiling kettle and the hum of the radio keeping loneliness away. The empty roads, the fields of sheep, the chickens waiting for a handful of oats. The dark clouds circling overhead forced him to hang his wet socks by the fireside to dry. Lurking in the shadow of his mind were dreams of abandoning the home he'd once loved with his beloved Peg and never returning. He could explore the world. He'd be happy doing so. Even if their swindle was uncovered, it might still be better than returning to an empty house deep in the Sligo countryside.

"I'm in," he shouted suddenly. The others smiled in agreement.

Springing to his feet, beads of sweat on his forehead, Moriarity took control, revealing more of the details of his scheme.

"I'll ring Mary and tell her I've had a tip-off that the revenue commissioners will carry out a surprise raid on bookmakers with outstanding taxes. Knowing her, she'll run for cover. She won't want to get caught red-handed. And then, my friends, her betting stall will be left abandoned. There's where we come in. We take it over for the day. And put my plan into action."

Silence descended upon the group momentarily. But their mouths popped open when Moriarity pulled his silk from his bag and announced, "With me sporting this attire, and twenty glorious race wins under my belt, rest assured, gentlemen, we'll attract plenty of attention."

"Jesus," exclaimed Walsh.

"Another round?" said Muldoon.

"With chasers," added McGowan. "And make them Jameson's."

After settling into their drinks, Bradshaw turned to Moriarity. "So, tell us, how did you come to know this wan Jackie so well then?"

"Shared bouts of sweat-soaked sex for a time in the city. But it wasn't long before it all wore off. Between drinking, sex, and gambling we began to hate the greedy, unwashed stench of one another. So, one morning, with surprisingly little difficulty, except for my empty wallet, I left her in the Great Southern Hotel – with the bill I might add. I wanted to sort myself out. But I learned the tricks of her trade, drinking whiskey neat, walking hand in hand along the harbour."

"Christ, fair dues, ye have the inside track," replied Bradshaw.

"True enough. Now, we've a bit more planning to do," continued Moriarity. "Are ye's in?"

"Let's go for it," said Walsh.

"I'm in," shouted McGowan and Muldoon almost in harmony. "What's next?"

"Listen up, lads, no more drinks from here on," Moriarity declared firmly.

His statement was met with puzzled expressions, even surprising himself with the directive he had just uttered. Straightening his lean frame, a surge of confidence seemed to well up within him as he outlined the intricate details of his plan. He delved into each task meticulously, from understanding the betting nuances to timing, placing wagers, and selecting the most favourable odds.

Once he had finished, he glanced at each man,

observing the expression on their faces. There was an unmistakable gleam of excitement, a sense of anticipation that seemed to intoxicate them all. It was as if they collectively believed that their final endeavour at Ballybrit could potentially yield a golden windfall for each of them.

Suddenly, Walsh's hand shot up. "Just one question. Why use a potato sack? It'll look ridiculous."

"When it's full of dosh instead of spuds, it won't. No one robs a potato sack, trust me. There's clerics and politicians, poets and ploughmen, singers and swingers, syndicates and celebrities, dreamers, and oceans of hucksters at the races, all with one goal - the reward of a winning bet and a big wad of money to show off. No one is above brandishing their winnings, but no one will walk away holding a potato sack."

"Fucking brilliant," gasped Walsh, gazing with newfound awe at his brother-in-law. He wondered how he hadn't seen this side of him before and vowed to tell Sheila that her husband mightn't be the scoundrel they brandished him after all. He even considered that they might have been a bit harsh on him by running to Uncle Jimmy in the nursing home with stories of his cavorting.

**

From the minute Moriarity appeared in his silk and launched into his lively banter, the betting stall began to throb with activity.

With his command of racing jargon and his eloquent demeanour, he took on the role of a preacher addressing his captivated congregation, assuming the mantle of a seasoned racecourse bookmaker effortlessly. To Walsh, he seemed a genius in action. Assisting in securing the winnings was the greatest thrill he had experienced since leaving the force — perhaps even eclipsing every other high in his entire life.

Observing his brother-in-law placing bets on a winning horse after the race had concluded and wagering on every horse in the last two races to guarantee success with the first four winners brought immense joy. Moriarity even began offering punters a stake in the winning horse, demanding a minimum buy-in of five thousand euros. Unbeknownst to them, upon their return to collect their winnings, the betting booth and its attendants would have vanished without a trace.

Their potato sacks brimming with cash, they hurriedly departed from the racecourse, dispersing in different directions, agreeing to reconvene later to divvy up their ill-gotten gains. And then, Moriarity found himself standing outside O'Connell's Bar in Eyre Square, resembling an army general eagerly awaiting the triumphant return of his victorious troops. As they assembled, he warmly shook each of their hands, effusively praising them for their meticulous execution of his instructions.

"Our paths may never cross again, lads, but what a pleasure it has been to collaborate with you," he said. "What a coup we've just pulled off!"

"You're a legend, Moriarity, an absolute legend," shouted Walsh. It was the first occasion he ever remembered heaping words of praise on him.

"Jesus Christ, I never saw anything like it in me life," chimed Muldoon. "You've got the gift of the gab for sure."

"The buzz was mighty," added McGowan. "Da'ya think we could get ever away with it again?"

"No way," said Bradshaw. "We're lucky to have gotten away scot free. Only a mad bunch of Paddy's would even have attempted it."

Stepping into the pub where the winnings were scheduled to be distributed, Moriarity assumed command once more. "Listen up, lads," his voice hushed and urgent. "We've got to move quick on this.

I'll snag your bags and head into the gents'. When I come out, you discreetly take them off me and scatter, different directions. Keep it casual, don't look back, and for God's sake, don't raise any suspicion, alright?"

***

Later, as Donnie Walsh hurried home, his heart pounded with anticipation. Anxious to stash the cash away from prying eyes, he dashed upstairs, clutching the potato sack tightly. Before tucking the money out of sight, he decided to steal a quick glance at his unexpected fortune. However, as he untied the sack, a wave of shock washed over him, draining the colour from his face.

His grip tightened on the wardrobe, attempting to steady himself, while his insides roiled. What he expected to be a pile of cash turned out to be a heap of neatly wrapped toilet rolls.

Fury surged through him, causing him to pace the room, fists clenched in frustration. Had his brother-in-law tricked and betrayed him? What recourse did he have? Alert the authorities? But that would only implicate himself. What purpose would it serve? His mind raced with these thoughts until he abruptly halted. The idea of confronting Moriarity, the thought of enduring the conman's scorn for falling prey to such a simple ruse, was unbearable. Pressing his palms to his eyes, he erupted into laughter. The sheer absurdity of it all struck him. Perhaps it was the best joke he'd encountered in ages — too long, indeed. Maybe he owed Moriarity something for the entertainment. Perhaps forgiveness was in order after all.

Ned Muldoon walked into Quinn's in Fenagh, a lopsided grin plastered on his face, his old bag slung casually over his shoulder. As he approached the bar, a glint of mischief danced in his eyes. With an air of theatricality, he slung the bag onto the counter, causing the contents to spill out dramatically.

Pulled out from the depths of the bag were what seemed like rolls of banknotes, which cascaded onto the counter, creating a visual spectacle that turned heads in the pub. Ned chuckled as he watched the effect unfold. Gleefully, he gestured to the barman, announcing, "Drinks on me, lads!"

The regulars' eyes widened in disbelief at the apparent windfall, and a chorus of surprised exclamations filled the pub. Glasses clinked and laughter erupted as everyone raised a toast to Ned. In the midst of the revelry, he regaled them with the story of his day at the Galway races, narrating the twists and turns with animated gusto. He had cleverly concealed the truth about the bag's actual contents, weaving an entertaining tale that painted him as the hero of his own thrilling adventure.

Amidst the storytelling and joyous camaraderie, the rolls of banknotes taken from under his own bed for showmanship soon made their way back into the bag, mysteriously disappearing beneath the toilet rolls at the bottom. A full round of drinks had cost him dearly as the patrons seized the opportunity to revel in the generosity, ordering rounds of doubles and chasers, knowing full well that it was Ned who was footing the bill.

Ned became the talk of Quinn's again that evening, the hero who had seemingly brought an unexpected windfall to the pub, leaving the locals amused and entertained once more by his colourful tale.

Meanwhile, in Sligo, Sean McGowan returned to his solitary house after the eventful day at the races. The dream of escape and a new beginning, nurtured with the hopes of leaving behind the lonesomeness that followed Peg's passing, had crumbled to dust. As he examined the toilet rolls in disbelief, a sense of deep disappointment and resignation washed over him. The opportunity to break free from the shackles of solitude, which had seemed within his grasp, had vanished, leaving behind a hollow void. It was a crushing blow to the aspirations he had dared to nurture, a stark reminder of life's unpredictability and its knack for dashing hopes.

***

Meanwhile, Moriarity, having returned to the racetrack, heard a familiar voice behind him.

"Nice work, my friend."

"Shit," he said angrily, louder than he'd meant to. The sharp voice belonged to none other than Jackie, his old shagging partner and stall owner. Alarmed, he swung round to see her thunderous face.

"Hand that bag over, you little bastard!"

What had he been thinking? How could he have imagined Jackie leaving the races over a warning about a tax inspection? Of course, she'd stayed. And monitored her stall from a distance. She'd witnessed the whole goings-on.

Cornered by two imposing henchmen, Moriarity reluctantly handed over the bag to Jackie, a last-ditch attempt at a turn in their relationship, hoping that perhaps now, with all his newfound winnings, she might take a chance on him.

"Jackie, could this be our chance? We could have a

fresh start, a place of our own," he ventured, a hint of hope in his voice.

Her response was far from what he expected. Snatching the sack of cash with force, she hurled a handful of notes at him.

"Take it! It's more than you're worth, you worthless piece of trash. You and me? That would've been a one-way ticket to a lifetime of misery," she spat, venom lacing her words.

Shocked by her reaction, Moriarity staggered backward, staring at the scattered bills strewn across the ground. The dream he'd envisioned was shattered, and the reality of his miscalculation hit like a thundering blow to the head. He stood there, frozen in disbelief, as the henchmen loomed ominously, their expressions betraying no hint of sympathy.

Standing in grim silence, Moriarity felt himself collapse like a pile of broken stones, the hopeless inadequacy of his life taking hold as he accepted the unsolvable mystery of how the full expectation of disaster never failed to materialise in his life.

Tucking his hands deep into the fur-lined pockets of his weathered overcoat, he wandered aimlessly amidst the vibrant throng that engulfed the Galway Races. The air buzzed with the animated chatter of patrons, their voices blending into an eclectic symphony against the backdrop of clinking glasses and spirited laughter. The kaleidoscope of colours and patterns, from finely woven tweed jackets to flamboyant hats bedecked with feathers and ribbons, painted a portrait of sartorial extravagance.

Careful to avoid the gaze of those he might have swindled earlier, he navigated the lively crowd, his head bowed to shield himself from recognition amidst the fluid sea of elegantly attired punters. Each face, a canvas of anticipation and thrill, bore traces of indulgence and excitement, marked by the remnants of lipstick stains on champagne flutes and the faint aroma of cigars wafting through the air.

Everywhere he turned, the atmosphere was alive with animated gestures, armfuls of racing forms, and high-pitched conversations punctuated by raucous cheers and impassioned exclamations. Women donned exquisitely tailored dresses in vibrant hues, the swish of their skirts creating a rhythm that danced in harmony with the lively racecourse ambiance.

From the resplendent marquees to the bustling paddocks, the aura was one of palpable exhilaration, punctuated by the crescendo of hooves thundering down the tracks. The subtle murmur of the crowd swelled into a unified roar as the horses bolted down the stretch, their determined gallop setting hearts racing and bets hanging in the balance.

And amidst this whirlwind of excitement and opulence, he, a solitary figure, moved with the crowd, a silent observer amidst the uproarious revelry, mindful to avoid any inadvertent acknowledgment by those he might have outfoxed just hours earlier.

As he ambled away from the track, the backdrop transformed into a picturesque panorama. Rolling hills embraced the racecourse, their slopes dotted with a patchwork of emerald-green fields. The distant call of seagulls hinted at Galway's proximity to the coast, and a soft breeze carried a hint of salt in the air. Beyond the bustle of the racetrack, the bus home awaited.

Against all odds, against the evidence of his life to date, and against pure reason, he took one final shot at life's unpredictable game and waited with that old familiar flutter of excitement. Later, in a spectacular absence of fanfare, he faced once again that tormented road to nowhere.

With nothing else to turn to, he sought solace in the fiery embrace of a few quick swigs of poitín, the illicit warmth coursing through his veins like a bittersweet remedy. The dimly lit pub offered a refuge, the air heavy with the aroma of rich, dark pints that beckoned like old friends.

In the intimate dance between the glass and his lips, he sought a fleeting escape into a surreal sense of forgetfulness and peace. The world outside the pub, with its burdens and sorrows, faded into the background, replaced by the amber glow of solace in each sip. For those stolen moments, he found respite from the complexities that tethered him.

Then, with the taste of poitín lingering on his tongue and the weight of dark pints settling in his chest, he left behind his last chance saloon and stepped onto the bus once more. Back to the life he knew best.

Mary Heeran White is Irish, living in County Clare with her husband, two daughters, and cherished dog, Cassie. Hailing from Leitrim, her diverse background encompasses a three-decade career in banking and entrepreneurial ventures. Re-kindling her passion for writing, her extensive professional journey provided rich fodder for her storytelling. Holding an MA in creative writing, Mary captures narratives of characters interwoven within the diverse fabric of Irish society.

In her forthcoming novel, *Falling for Zac – An Intercultural Love Story*, Mary navigates the challenging journey of an immigrant pursuing his promised land. When refugee Zac falls in love on Irish shores, he unwittingly becomes embroiled in complex challenges posed by cultural and religious disparities.

Awaiting publication, her debut novel *Memoir of a Whistleblower* delves into the intricate world of love, deceit, and betrayal. As banker Cathy O'Donnell falls for David Malone, a beguiling Solicitor who shrewdly manipulates legal documents to swindle millions from banks, she faces moral dilemmas with damning consequences.

You can find Mary at:
Mary Heeran White on Facebook and LinkedIn
@heeranwhite on Instagram
@MaryWhiteAuthor on Twitter

www.ingramcontent.com/pod-product-compliance
Lightning Source LLC
Chambersburg PA
CBHW031125210626
46816CB00016B/2373